Stripped
by Love

Mahagony Redd

ChocolateRoze Publishing

Cover Design: creationbydonna.com

Interior Design and Typesetting: interiorbookdesigns.com

ISBN 978-0-9884712-3-8

Sending My Love and Appreciation

First of all, I would like to thank GOD for giving me the strength to get through all my struggles and pain. Sending my love to my mother, Bernice Forrest. "I got dirt in my eyes" — that's an inside joke. My children, Maliya and Derrick Grinnage: thanks for being the best children a parent could ever ask for. To my divas (Tawana Ellerbe, Mecca Forrest, Kim Worrell, and Shamekia Houston and to my manager Anneka Davis): I got nothing but love for you ladies. To my nana Audrey Grinnage the Virginia Diva. To my brother Robert aka Boom thanks for waiting until I completed the book to read it. To my best friend Juanita Da Queen. To my girl Tawana Tanique Black Butterfly, Jeanette Sapphire, Author Vytamin Voice, Lakeisha Nicole Hammonds, Blossom, Char Mayo and Marcia Neal; also to Devon Parham I'm so proud of you cuz....Earnest J. Anderson Jr and Kevin Neale and Lowrns Hazegod. To my children, Sheyannie Smith and Naim Hayes. To my other half, the reason for my writing this book, my supporter, my Boo-Bear I love you. To Keron Bryan- my photographer you did a great job. To Sheila, Russell, Junie, Leon, Buster, uncle Kym and Sharon.

I want to send my love to my entire Forrest and Grinnage family. To all my friends and supporters and everyone who had faith in me and to those who encouraged me to stay focused no matter how hard things may have gotten. Smooches....

This is dedicated to one of the most beautiful women I had the pleasure of knowing, my grandmother Florie Forrest aka Flo-Jo. R.I.P. Grandma. You will always be in my heart and I know you are watching over my Angel-Boo.

Chapter 1

Karma

Damn, I thought to myself as I rolled over and looked at this piece-of-shit baby daddy of mines. Just looking at this broke-ass-nigga turned my stomach—years of a wasted fuck. Here I was, a beautiful black woman, and I was sleeping head-to-foot with this fake-ass-nigga. Why didn't I follow my gut instinct and leave his ass a long time ago?

He better not come up here wanting no pussy with his tired-ass dick. I can't stand his sex game; he is straight-up whack.

Who was the real asshole?

Me—I was the one lying next to the motherfucker. I was the one that fucked him every night, even though I was not satisfied. We had a beautiful daughter together. I loved my daughter to death, but she deserved a better father. He swears he's such a good dad. Let him tell it, he deserves the Father of the Year award.

My trouble with guys began when I was young and dumb and out of control. I met Jorrell, my baby daddy, in my late teens, but he wasn't my first. My first, Jermaine (a.k.a. Jay), was a deadbeat in every other way possible. He was a piece of shit, too, but I was young, and once I got a piece of the dick, I didn't know how to act.

All my girls had lost their virginity; I was the only one left. I tried but couldn't get what the "BIG" talk was about. I didn't feel the pain they said I would feel. So now what? My virginity was gone; what happens next? After having sex with Jermaine, that asshole told me straight-up—I belonged to him. I thought it was cute at first. I felt important, special. I soon found out he meant that literally. When I got out of school, he would be sitting on the hood of his car, waiting for me. I liked that; it made me feel like the fly chick. He was older, driving, and about his business, which was robbing motherfuckers for whatever money, jewelry, drugs, and any other thing he could catch a nigga for. I did't know any better. I should have, but I didn't care, not until he started busting me upside my head.

I looked on the dresser and noticed a picture lying face down. Once I looked at the picture I already knew it was about to go down.

"Who the fuck is this, Jay?" I yelled as he laid there pretending to be asleep. "Wake the fuck up. Who is this? You know I'm really tired of your shit, Jay." I looked at him, thinking, *I can't stand your fucking ass.* I wanted to stab this motherfucker, but I didn't want to go to jail for attempted murder—or murder, for that matter.

"What?" he yelled. What, bitch? Get the fuck out of here—take your ass home."

I started laughing to myself. *Yeah, his bitch ass is gonna wake the fuck up.* I went to fill up a bucket with cold water. I called to him again. "Jay, who the fuck is this bitch you hugged up with in this picture?"

He refused to answer, so I threw the water on him. As soon as that freezing cold water hit him, he jumped up, and started tugging at his wet boxers.

"What the fuck you doing, Taraine?" he yelled as he wiped the water from his face.

Next thing I knew, this bastard slapped the shit out of me. "Why the fuck did you hit me, motherfucker?" I yelled, holding my face.

"You're a dumb bitch."

"Why the fuck did you just hit me?" I didn't give one thought about the fact that I'd just drenched this asshole with freezing cold water. All I wanted to know was who the hell he was hugged up with in the picture. My face felt like it was on fire. "Who is this, Jay?"

"Get the fuck out my face with your dumb shit."

"You fucking this bitch?"

"No," he answered.

"I'm going to ask you one more time. Are you fucking her?"

"No, you dumb bitch. You better clean this fucking room up," he yelled as he reached under his mattress and pulled out his .45. "I should beat the shit out of you."

"I ain't cleaning shit!" I yelled. "I'm tired of your shit, Jay." Next thing I knew, this motherfucker had his hands around my neck.

"Taraine, you- a- dumb-ass bitch."

"Get off me — I can't breathe." I think I started turning blue in the face. I was trying to say sorry, but the words wouldn't come out. He refused to let me go. While choking my neck, he pulled up my shirt and began sucking on my nipple.

"What you want to know, Taraine?" he asked as he slowly removed his hands from my neck. "You want to know if I fucked that bitch? That's what you want to know, right? Damn, Taraine, why the fuck are you bugging out? Don't you know how much I love you? I don't care who I fuck. You're mine. Don't I fuck you good?" He asked

As the tears rolled down my face, I answered, "Yes, but why, Jay? Why?"

"Cause I can do that. That bitch don't mean shit to me." He sat me on top of the dresser and started fucking me. I thought, *Bitch, you're so fucking stupid.* Then he went down and ate my pussy like it was his last dinner, making my juices flow like a water fountain. This man had just threatened to beat the shit out of me with his .45, and I'm letting him have his way with me. I wanted to take that .45 and blow his fucking head off as he ate away; making this the last pussy he ever put his lips on. Then he rose up and slid the dick in me again.

"Taraine, I love you, girl." He ain't that big but the sex was so intense, it began to feel as if he was busting my shit open. He squeezed me tight as he released all up in me. Then he looked at me and said, "Know your position, Taraine. Know your fucking position. Now clean my shit, and take your ass home."

I cleaned up, and as I was getting ready to leave, I looked in the mirror and realized my eye was turning purple. How the fuck can I go home like this? I lived in Albany projects with my grandparents, my mother and five other people; somebody would notice I had a black eye. "Look at my eye, Jay."

He looked at me and said, "You'll be all right."

I managed to cover up my black eye with some foundation my mother had in her make-up kit. It worked perfectly—that's what I used to hide the hickeys he put on my face and neck.

When I got home, everything was good. Of course, my mother and no one else in the house recognized the black eye Jay had put there. Damn shame; if only they knew the bullshit I was going through at such a young age.

Of course, the fighting continued, the bitches continued, and I continued to stay in this out-of-control abusive relationship. On top of everything, I was pregnant—fifteen and pregnant. *Damn!*

Yeah, I was fifteen—and running around like I was grown. Fifteen and fighting every other day with this bastard. Oh, I fought back but never really won.

I thought I was tough, but he was tougher. Was it his look that made me act like such as ass? It wasn't just about sex. Maybe it was just my own insecurities. All of my friends had boyfriends—maybe I didn't want to be the only one without a man, even if my so-called man didn't give a fuck about me. I was a beautiful girl with a nice body, and I dressed real nice, but that still didn't stop him from cheating on me.

Damn, I can't tell my mother I'm pregnant. I'll really get my ass kicked. I decided to skipped school the next day. I needed to go and talk to Jay about our situation.

When Jay opened the door he was dressed and ready to go out and get into his usual routine. My heart was racing as I walked into the house. I wasn't sure how he would react to the news I had for him.

"Jay, I'm pregnant."

"No, you ain't!" he yelled.

"For real, Jay. I'm pregnant.

"Well, I got the money. You know what to do."

"Money," I said. "I don't need any money because I'm keeping my baby."

"No, the fuck you ain't. This ain't no time for me and no babies right now, and please don't start that crying shit."

I wanted to have this baby, and he wanted to continue playing the club, fucking bitches, and robbing niggas.

Later on that night, he woke me up. "I'm going to the club tonight so I'm taking you home." He drove my ass right to the parking lot. "Go upstairs!" he yelled as he looked at me, sitting with my arms crossed. "Come on now. Stop playing. I got to go and pick my man up."

"Well, I'm going with you."

"Bitch, if you don't stop playing ..."

"If I don't stop playing *what?* What you gonna do, Jay? Hit me?" I said, gripping my stomach.

"I don't give a fuck about that baby, and you ain't keeping it," he said.

"Well, I decided I am."

"Well, I decided you're not, and if you don't get the fuck out my car, I'm going to call your mother downstairs and tell her your dumb ass is pregnant."

"Shut the fuck up. You ain't going to tell her shit."

I lived on the second floor, facing the parking lot. I guess we were real loud because the next thing I knew, my mother was walking toward the car.

"What are you doing, Taraine?"

"Nothing," I said with an attitude.

"If the man wants to go about his business, let him go."

"No, I'm not getting out."

"Ms. Debra, your daughter is pregnant."

"What?" my mother said.

"She's pregnant. I told her if she doesn't get out of my car, I was going to let you know she's pregnant."

My mother looked at me as if she was ready to kill me.

"Get out of the car, Taraine."

I still didn't move.

"Get out of the damn car, now." She yelled.

I just gave him a look: *You bitch-ass. All this, just to go to a club and rub up on some ass, huh? You sold me out.*

"Fuck you," I said as I got out of his car. I tried to break the door off as I slammed it shut. My mother stormed into the building; I walked behind her. I was both ashamed and embarrassed but more so angry with that motherfucker.

Early the next morning came "the talk." My mother asked me, "So what are you going to do, Taraine?"

"Keep it," I said.

"Why?"

"Because I love him."

"No. You think you love him. He told me you were pregnant because you wouldn't get out of his car. That boy ain't interested in having no baby. How much love do you think he have for you? He is no good for you, and every time someone tries to drill that into your hard head, you look at them as if they don't have a clue as to what they're talking about. You don't know anything about love, because if you did, you would see that man don't love you at all. You're depriving yourself of so much, being involved with him. He's an idiot."

In my mind, I was thinking, *whatever. You don't know anything about this love/hate relationship we got going on.* I looked at my mom as the tears filled my eyes. I was blindsided by reality. I know what she was saying was the truth. I just wasn't in the mood to hear it. I just wanted to get back in my bed and sleep so I didn't have to think about this situation any longer.

Monday morning came fast, and I couldn't wait to leave for school—but really, I wanted to leave to go bang down his door. He probably got some bitch up in there that he brought home from the club over the weekend.

I knocked on the door and rang the bell. "Jay, open the fucking door. I know you're in there." No answer, so I started banging harder. He finally opened the door. "Why you do me like this, Jay? That's some bitch-ass shit you did to me the other night." As I walked down the hall to his bedroom, my voice escalated just in case some dumb broad was inside. I was in fighting mode and ready for anything to pop off. To my surprise, nobody was in there. I should have come yesterday, but I was too upset to fight with anybody, including Jay.

I was happy as hell. I ain't have to fuck a bitch up early in the morning. Yeah, I'm young, but I get down for mines. I'll beat a bitch ass with no problem, without a care in the world. Just like the time Jay was chasing me around the house with a knife. I got one of his mother's frying pans and tried to knock his fucking head off. I guess after getting my ass kicked so much, I started fighting hard without thinking about the consequences.

I got in his bed. "I'm not going to school today. I don't feel like it. Plus, we need to talk. I told my mother I was having the baby, and she wasn't having it. So, when you give me the money, I'll have the abortion, even though it's not what I want."

All of a sudden, he started yelling, "You ain't killing my seed!"

I looked at this fool like he's crazy. "Ain't you the same motherfucker who said you not ready for no baby right now? What kind of shit you smoking, Jay?"

"I'm dead serious," he said. He climbed on top of me as if he was about to start kissing me, but he started choking the shit out of me.

"Get off me! What's wrong with you?"

"You ain't getting rid of my seed that's word to everything I love."

"Whatever you say. Just get the fuck off me. Damn, you're bugging."

Before I knew it, we were getting it in, and I was happy, thinking, *Yes, I got him. I got him right where I want him.*

I didn't go home for days. My mother called his house, looking for me, but I told him to tell her I wasn't there. Where else would I be? She knew I was there, and I knew she was going to kill me, but I was trying to keep my man.

As we laid there sleeping, I was in heaven; it felt so good. I rubbed my belly and thought about our future and how this baby would keep us together.

Then the phone rang. I laid still and acted as if I was asleep. Jay picked up the phone. "Yo, what up?"

I could hear the sound of a female voice, but I couldn't understand what she was saying.

He hung up. I continued to lie still, so he'd think I was still asleep. He tried to quietly slide out of bed and get dressed. *This bastard thinks I'm so fucking stupid,* I thought. *I'll wait until he's ready to walk out the door; then I'll blow his ass the fuck up.*

As soon as he reached to open the door, I jumped up. "Where the fuck are you going?"

"Oh, Shawn just called. He wants me to meet him up the block."

Shawn was his brother. "No, that wasn't no damn Shawn that just called you. I heard some dumb-ass bitch on the phone. Your dumb ass ain't leaving this house." I begin putting my shit on, getting into fight mode.

"Yo, not right now, Taraine. I'll be right back."

"No, fuck that we will be right back."

He left out the bedroom, and I was right behind.

"Here you go with the dumb shit again," he said.

"Well, we'll be dumb together, motherfucker. I'm tired of your shit, for real, Jay," I yelled.

We got to the steps in his building, and the motherfucker pushed me down the stairs. My face hit the railing, and all I felt was blood sliding down my face. I got up and ran back up the steps. I charged at him and began punching him in his face. The next thing I knew, I was falling backwards down the steps.

"You stupid bitch, I told you to let me go." He ran down the steps and started kicking me in my stomach.

"Jay, the baby!" I yelled, but he was so out of control, it seemed as if he couldn't even hear my cries. I felt myself cramping up as I tried to cover my face and stomach at the same time. He finally stopped, then spit on me. "Stupid bitch! You dumb bitch. Fuck you. I do what I want, go where I want, and fuck who I want!" he yelled as he walked down the steps.

I tried to get up, but the pain was to excruciating. My stomach was cramping; I began to feel like I was peeing on myself. I put my hands between my thighs and realized I wasn't peeing; I was bleeding. I begin screaming for help, but nobody came. I pulled myself up by holding on to the step railing. Once I was on my feet, I felt the blood sliding heavily down my legs. I wasn't too sure what was going on but I prayed I wasn't having a miscarriage. As I slowly walked down the steps, I felt as if I was going to pass out. I thought, *Why, Jay? All this for some pussy, when you had pussy lying right next to you.* The pain was so bad, but my fear of me losing my baby didn't allow me to shed a tear. I stumbled down the steps until I got outside. There was not a soul in sight. I got to the corner of his block and still saw no one. I continued walking, and then I heard him calling my name. I tried to speed up my walk but couldn't. *This man had completely lost his mind; he is trying to finish me off,* I thought. I wanted to run but couldn't. When I reached the next corner I saw two people coming towards me, so I fell to the ground. I tried my best not to move, so they would think I was unconscious and call for help.

Jay finally caught up to me and yelled my name, like he was concerned.

"Taraine"

I guess he noticed the two people coming toward me as well.

"Who did this to you?"

I wanted to scream, "*You*, motherfucker! *You* did this to me. I hate you, you fucking bastard." *Why did you do this to me? I loved you with all my heart.* Eventually, the police and the ambulance came, and by then, he was nowhere in sight. I was taken to St. John's Hospital. Unfortunately, I lost the baby. I was hurt and confused—young and in love with a man who never really loved me at all. I was an out-of-control teenager who he could control. The police questioned me, but I didn't have the courage to turn Jay in to the police. After all, I still loved him. *He's sorry; I know he is*—that's what I tried to convince myself of.

When my mother showed up, she immediately said, "Jay did this to you."

I said, "No, Debra, he didn't."

"You can protect him all you want; he'll get what's coming to him."

I just wanted her to go away, and then I thought to myself, *where the fuck is Jay? Probably fucking some next bitch.*

I was in the hospital for a couple of days. *Wait until I see him, dumb motherfucker.* My mother held me down; she showed me so much love. How could I have been so naïve about my situation?

"Why did he kill my baby?" I said as I closed my eyes and cried silently. I felt like nobody understood. I didn't even understand, because in my heart, I still wanted to see him. I missed him so fucking much. A part of him was no longer growing inside of me.

The following Monday I got up for school. To get to my school I had to pass Jay's house. The closer I got to his building, the harder my heart pumped. To my surprise, Jay stepped out of the building as I approached it, but before I could react, some chick stepped out behind him. He wrapped his arm around the girl and walked toward his car, as if he didn't even see me.

What do I do? What do I say? Before I could get my thoughts together, he jumped in his car and pulled off. I stood there, shocked by what had just happened, and I began to cry. I couldn't move; I felt paralyzed. I'd lost my baby and my man.

Why did I follow behind him when he'd tried to leave? I blamed the whole situation on myself. The pain and the ignorance were blocking the reality of Jay being a piece of shit, and I never should have been with him in the first place. He was only about his needs and wants, and I just couldn't see that. Throughout all the ass whippings, the cheating, even the miscarriage, I didn't want to allow myself to believe he didn't love me.

I tried to get myself together the best way I could and proceeded on to school. When I got to school, it seemed like all eyes were on me. Was it just my imagination? No, it wasn't, so I left but didn't have anywhere to go. I went to my best friend, Lisa's, house, but I hadn't kicked it with her since I started being with

Jay. Lisa always pretended to go to school; she would wait for her mother to leave for work, then go back home, so I knew she was home, but would she let me in? I knocked on the door. She opened it with a look on her face like, "what you want, bitch?"

"Can I talk to you, Lisa?"

"About what?" she said.

I guess the look on my face made her feel sorry for me, and she invited me inside. She'd never liked Jay, but she didn't go through the I-told-you-so routine; she just listened to me like a real friend would. Talking to her kind of put things back into perspective for me. I knew it was going to be hard to get through the pain, but I was glad I had a friend like her to count on.

<><><>

My focus was getting back into school and being the young woman I was before I met Jay. Soon enough, I found myself back to chilling with my girls and making fun of the young-ass boys that thought they were saying something. I thought to myself, *it beats getting my ass kicked every day.*

I did miss Jay a little—or did I just miss being under a so-called man.

Two weeks later, I heard that Jay was found behind the back of an alley in Harlem, with one shot to the back of his head. Whoever shot him didn't even rob him. They said he had, like, ten thousand dollars in his pocket, and he still had on all his jewelry. I guess karma is a bitch—all that shit he did to people, and all that shit he did to me came back and bit him in the ass.

Well, rest in hell, motherfucker. Payback is a bitch.

Chapter 2

Mommy's Baby Daddy's Maybe

I started doing well in school, but I missed out on so much. In order for me to graduate on time, I had to transfer to an alternative high school. I made the transfer, but I still didn't graduate on time. I had to go to summer school. That was okay; I completed summer school and got my high school diploma.

I decided to take a break from the books, so when the fall came, I didn't go to college—dumb-ass move.

Now I found myself in the streets all the time with my friends. I started dating again, but I didn't really get to serious with anyone. One guy I met was a big-time hustler in the PJs. He would take me up to his apartment, kiss me and suck on me, and get me all in the mood; then rub and hump on me or make me stroke his dick until he came. When we walked out of his building, his boys would be standing there, and he'd give them this look, as if he'd just fucked the shit out of me. I would be thinking, *little do y'all know your boy is scared of pussy.* He could have stroked his own fucking dick; wasting my damn time.

Big-time Will was scared of pussy—what a fucking joke. He liked to buy me nice things, though, so I continued stroking his short fat dick.

Then there was this other guy they called B-Boy, but before we could get into a real relationship, he was killed in a motorcycle accident. He was so cool, but all he used to tell me was how I could make good money being a stripper. Thanks, but no thanks—that's not an option for me. B-Boy was obsessed with motorcycles; he was in love with them. No one could believe it when they found out he was in an accident. Every time I closed my eyes, all I would see is his beautiful smile as he laughed and tried to convince me that I could "get paid" off my breasts alone. "Yo, you could really make some paper doing this shit, Tee," he would say. "I'm telling you—motherfuckers will go crazy off your big-ass tits."

I miss you, B-Boy. Rest In Peace.

<><><>

My mom finally decided to move out of my grandparents' apartment. Throughout the process of moving, I met who I thought was going to be my future husband, but he turned out to be the biggest loser ever. I was walking down the block, trying to ignore the hissing sound of someone trying to get my attention. He continued hissing, so I turned around to give him a disgusted look that said, "Oh, *please*."

He yelled, "Can I get two minutes of your time, good-looking?" I paid his ass no mind and kept it moving—until I bumped into this kid I went to school with named Sin, or Sincere.

"What's going on, Tee?"

"What you been up to?"

Before we could strike up a conversation, this two-minute motherfucker was right on my ass. "What's up, Ma? Can I get two minutes of your time?" I wasn't trying to give him no play, but he wasn't trying to give up. "What's your name, yo?"

"What's my name?" I repeated as I looked around to see who the fuck he was talking to.

"What's your name?" he said again.

"Why?" I said.

"Because I want to get to know you."

"Is that right?" I said sarcastically.

"You right, Ma; the right one for me."

"My name is Taraine. What's yours?"

"Jorrell, but my boys call me Rell."

I thought, *Okay, we exchanged names. Now break the fuck out.* He looked nothing like Jay; he was the total opposite—dark skin, short and skinny, with a wide nose. Plus, it didn't even look like he had a ride.

"So can I get your number?" he asked.

"For what?"

"So I can call you sometime. I want to get to know you; get into a little entertainment."

"What do you mean by a little entertainment?"

"Like I said, I want to get to know you. I want us to get to know each other."

I gave him my number. What the hell—I haven't really been in a serious relationship since Jay. Every guy that tried to kick it with me already had other women, and of course, they didn't let it be known. I didn't even ask him if he had a girl. He probably would have lied about it anyway, so fuck it.

The next morning my phone rang. "Hello."

"What's up, Ma?"

"Who is this?"

"It's Rell."

Just that fast, I'd forgotten I'd given him my number and to be honest, I wasn't expecting him to call. "Oh, what's up?"

"Can I come by to see you?"

"For what?" I asked.

"Just to talk, feel your vibe. You know, see if we got a connection. I'm trying to get to know you on a personal level."

"You can come through," I said, shaking my head. *What are you getting yourself into, bitch?* I gave him my address, and he said he'd reach me in about half an hour. When I hung up the phone, I said, "Half an hour? Nah, that motherfucker ain't got no ride."

My doorbell rang. I opened the door and standing in front of me was this fake-ass Ja Rule-looking motherfucker. Not my type, but he had a cuteness about him.

He came inside, and we got to kicking it. He told me how he hustled out of town. I was thinking, *you ain't really getting paper out there because you're walking. You ain't even driving a hoopty. He was probably nickel-and-diming it right on the corner where I met him, talking about he hustle out of town, like he doing big things—whatever.*

The more we talked, the cooler he seemed. I didn't know if he was keeping it real, but time would tell. I hadn't slept with anybody in a while, because all Will seem to like doing was jerking off.

Rell played the sweet gentleman role, and I fell for it. It felt kind of good to get some attention. Before he left, he asked me for a kiss on the cheek. *Fuck kissing me on the cheek. Give me some tongue, Boo. Let me see if you know how to work it. That will give me a little insight on how you eat pussy.* I thought.

He said, "I'll call you later," but before he walked down the steps, he turned around and said, "Yo, you got fifty dollars I could borrow until tomorrow?"

"What? Are you serious? You're kidding me right. What the fuck you mean, can you borrow fifty dollars?" That was strike two, but my dumb ass gave it to him. Of course, I didn't see him the next day nor did I hear from him, but that was cool. I didn't take it as a big loss. On the third day, I had made plans to go out with Big Will.

My phone rang. "I'm on my way," the voice on the phone said.

"All right, I'll be ready." Fifteen minutes later, my doorbell rang. I opened the door—and it was Rell.

"What's up, Ma?"

"What you doing here?"

"What?" he said. "I called just a minute ago and said I was on my way."

Oh, shit! I thought it was Big Will calling me. Damn, I'm bugging out.

We went to my bedroom, and I told him to relax and get comfortable. I went to unplug the phone, just in case Will decided to call. He always called before he came over. I went back into the room and sat next to him.

"You got my money?" I asked him, as if I was some type of mafia chick.

"Nah, but I got you."

"When, motherfucker, when?"

We looked at each other and started cracking up, but I was dead-ass serious about my fifty bucks. I needed a wrap and set and a manicure. He leaned toward me and started kissing me; then he started rubbing on my breast. It felt so good; it'd been a while since I felt a touch like that. Before I could even open my eyes, he pulled my panties to the side and started thrusting himself all up in me. My pussy was so tight; it felt as if I was a born-again virgin. The feeling was much different from when I actually lost my virginity. I wanted to scream, but I didn't. *Is this how it is supposed to feel? Is this the pain my girls said I was going to feel the first time I had sex?*

He started nibbling on my ear and sucking on my neck, working his way down to my nipples. He softly licked around my nipple until all of him was deep inside of me. Due to the fact it'd been a while, I couldn't tell if he was really packing, but it felt like it was at least eight inches, as his dick spread my shit wide open.

Within three days, I was open, and we were officially a couple, always on the go, always doing shit together, but most of all, always fucking. We fucked like rabbits, I was happy, and I was falling in love with this man. My mother seemed to like him—until that dreadful day when she walked in on us while he was deep in me. She slammed the door in shock.

Oh, shit, Rell! I was shitting bricks, but we both started laughing. I knew that *she* knew I'd been fucking—I was once pregnant—but she'd never seen me in action. We both got dressed and walked toward the living room. She was standing there at the front door with a bat in her hand, and she told Rell, "Don't you dare step in my house again, or you might not make it out!"

"All right, Ms. Debra."

Yeah, right, I thought.

After she closed the door, she gave me the business, but it went in one ear and out the other. The next morning, I was so slick as soon as my mother left for work, five minutes later my doorbell rang. I opened the door and to my surprise, Rell was standing there. "What's up, baby?" I said, giving him the biggest hug, as if I hadn't just seen him yesterday.

"Your mother is going to kill us."

"What she don't know won't hurt her," I said with a devilish smile on my face. We liked to fuck—where else would we be able to make it happen but at my house? After a while, we started going to the hotel. He would get his weed, Heineken, and food, and we'd go at it for eight hours plus. I gave head like a motherfucker; I was definitely good at my craft, which was sucking the skin of that dick. Then, one day I started teasing his balls with my tongue, rolling and twirling them all in my mouth. I had Rell screaming and moaning like a straight-up bitch. "Oh, Taraine, what you doing to a nigga?" I had already mastered jerking the dick from Big Will. My new goal was to make this man cry from this good head I was giving. I patted myself on the back because the way he was moaning, I guess it was a job well done. His head game was good but not as good as Jay's, but I could teach him what a bitch like me was use to. The only thing that would bother me from time to time about him was his height. He was a short guy, not really my type, but I was happy, so I looked past it. They say everyone is the same height in bed.

The bitches around his way couldn't stand me, and the guys always tried to holla—a bunch of broke motherfuckers getting high off their own supply. To be honest, Rell was the same way—he wasn't "'bout it." He had what he had, and that was it.

For days I didn't hear from Rell. I would go on his block, but he was nowhere to be found. I asked a couple of them where he was but I couldn't get no info. Finally, one guy who lived next door to him told me he got into it with some young kid on the block. They had a fight, and then the boy pulled out a gun and started blasting on him and chasing Rell through the streets.

"So where the hell is Rell at now?"

"That nigga in the house on the low," he said.

"Damn." *I'm fucking with a straight up bitch; he scared to hit the streets.* Before that situation, he had gotten into it with some other kid named Black for cutting his money short, that he had supposedly made out of town. That's when I started questioning his swag. I was really dealing with a clown, a push-over, a punk, a half-stepper, and most of all, a pussy.

He finally showed his face, but I didn't let him know I heard what had happened.

"Where the fuck have you been, Rell?"

"I'm sorry, Taraine. I had to go out of town to collect my money."

"So, we got money to spend, huh?"

"We?" he said.

"Yeah 'we."

I knew he was lying out his ass, but I didn't say shit. He was very popular on the streets without being a hustler, but I couldn't figure out why. One thing about him, you would never find him on the corner with a bunch of niggas, smoking and drinking. He did what he did; vibe with his boys, made his little bit of money, and then broke out. Like I always knew, he was nickel-and-dimer.

I later learned he did have a little bit of Jay in him. He used to rob people also, but let me be specific. He used to rob females, catching them for their earrings, chains, and bags. Most of all, what made them alike was they both had hand problems.

<><><>

I went to his house around one in the morning. I rang the bell and called him but couldn't reach him. I looked up at his window and noticed the lights were on, so I knew he was home. I thought, *Okay, I have to go and fuck a bitch up. Here we go again with all the bullshit; I'm not going through this shit again.* So I decided to leave. As I walked up the block I bumped into one of Jay boys, Cee. He talked a minute about Jay and how fucked up it was, the way he was killed. I didn't respond because if you don't have anything good to say, then don't say shit at all.

He said, "You looking good."

"Thank you."

"What you doing on the Ave?"

"I'm fucking with Rell from the Marks."

He looked at me with this weird look on his face and said, "Oh, word."

"Yeah, for a minute we've been kicking it." I said

All right, Cee, I'll see you around." I continued walking but before I could hit the corner, I was caught off guard by a slap to the face. This little fucker came up on me and bitch-slapped me. I held my cheek, trying to get it together and turned to Rell. "What the fuck did you slap me for?"

"Don't try to play me on the Ave, talking to that bitch-ass nigga."

"What the fuck are you talking about, Rell?"

"I saw you talking to Cee bitch ass."

"I know him, Rell. You're bugging out." This little fucker was out of control, and I was not trying to go back to the same old bullshit I went through with Jay, so I just walked away. "You're a fucking dickhead, Rell, and you call him a bitch ass. Why didn't you walk up on both of us and slap the shit out of him? You know why, Rell? Because you're a bitch," I said as I walked away from him.

"Whatever," he said.

"I know it's whatever, bitch. Lose my fucking number."

"Fuck you, Taraine."

"No, fuck you, Rell," I said as I kept it moving up the Ave. I'm not with the fighting anymore. I can do better than being with a man who thinks its okay to beat the shit out of a woman but wants to compromise with a man. Something's not right with that shit, and I ain't having it; fuck that.

The next morning he didn't call, and I surely didn't call him. Anyway, I was going to hang out with the girls, Fatima and Shantae, two crazy-ass bitches who just happen to be my cousins. As I waited downstairs for Fatima to pull up, I was praying Rell wouldn't come to my house. It seemed like forever, but these bitches finally pulled up, grinning from ear to ear.

"What's up, bitch?" Fatima yelled. Fatima was driving a cherry-red Lexus.

"It took y'all long enough."

"We went to pick up Kelly, but she changed her mind at the last minute."

"Why?" I asked.

Fatima said, "You know Keith is not letting that bitch out of his sight. I don't know why she's moving to North Carolina next month. They're going to get down there and act the fuck up. He's gonna be fucking her up, and then she's gonna be fucking his ass up; it's crazy. You know he calls the cops on her when she really starts to spazz out," Fatima said, laughing. "His ass gets scared to death, that's why he calls the cops on her."

"Yo, that shit is fucked up. How the fuck you calling the cops on your wifey? What does he say? My wife just beat my ass?"

We all started laughing. We didn't do too much, just a little shopping. That's one way to release stress — going shopping and buying shit you can't really afford, but buying it makes you feel so much better on the inside. It makes you forget about all the fucked up shit going on in your life, even if it's just for a little while.

After I got home from hanging with my girls, the phone rang. I was contemplating on if I should answer it or not. They always say to go with your gut instinct, which was telling me not to answer, but curiosity always kills the cat. And of course, I answered it.

"Yo, come down stairs."

"No. Fuck you, and don't call my house anymore!" I yelled and hung up the phone. Rell continuously called until I decided to shut the phone off. This man was not going to be aggravating me tonight — fuck that.

I got up the next morning, unsure of what the fuck to do. I was used to Rell coming over as soon as my mother left, or us going to a hotel and fucking all day long — damn, he's an idiot.

I made breakfast and the smell made me nauseous. "Oh, no, no, no!" I yelled as I ran down the hall to the bathroom. My doorbell rang, but I couldn't get up from the toilet bowl. I threw up, but all that came out was some kind of orange-looking liquid, as if I'd drunk some orange juice this morning. Someone still was ringing my doorbell, as if they knew I was home. I finally got up, rinsed out my mouth, and wiped off my face. I opened the door, and it was Rell standing there with a dozen of roses and candy. *So typical,* I thought, even though no man had ever done this before. *This motherfucker is just trying to get back in.*

"I don't want that shit, motherfucker. Good-bye," I said and slammed the door, dead in his face.

"I'm not leaving, Tee. We need to talk."

"No. You should have thought about that shit the other night."

"Ma, I'm sorry. Can I come in, please?"

On top of everything, Rell knew what type of relationship I'd previously had with Jay.

"No. You played yourself, Rell. Give that shit to some other bitch."

"I brought them for you, Ma. Open the door."

I hated when he called me Ma. I wasn't his fucking mother.

"I'm not leaving!" he yelled.

I waited for about half an hour. I looked through the peephole and he was still sitting there. *Damn, Rell, why can't you just leave like any ordinary person would?* I thought. I gave in and opened the door. "Why are you still here, Rell?"

"I'm feeling you, Taraine. I'm sorry for what happened on the Ave. Can I please come in to talk to you?"

"Whatever," I said, "but I don't want shit from you. You slapped me and that was fucked up."

"Nah, Tee, I didn't like what I saw, and I don't even like that dude. He's a clown."

"So why the fuck didn't you step to him? You didn't even approach us. You waited until I walked off, and then you stepped to me. That's some bitch-ass-shit. I'm not feeling that at all. No, fuck you, Rell. I don't need this right now."

"Come on, babe." He grabbed my arm and pulled me toward him.

"No, get the fuck off me." I just burst out crying. "I don't feel good, and I don't have time for this right now."

"What's wrong? Are you pregnant?"

"I don't know."

"Well, you need to check that out, and if you are, you know what we need to do."

"No, what's that, Rell?"

"Get rid of it," he said, so plain and simple. "I can't have NO more kids."

"What you mean, no more kids? I never knew you had any."

"Well, I do. I have a little girl, and she's two years old."

"And I'm just finding out about this? *Get the fuck out, mother-fucker!*" I yelled at the top of my lungs.

"I'm not leaving, Taraine. First of all, you're not even sure if you're pregnant."

I just started putting on my clothes so I could get far away from this man — or should I say asshole. "Leave my house, Rell."

"Ma, I'm sorry."

"And stop calling me your fucking ma. Do I look like your damn mother?"

"I'm not trying to hurt you," he said.

"You're not trying to hurt me. We've been together for a while now, and I didn't even know you had a daughter. Now I might be pregnant by you, and trust me, if I am, I'm not having an abortion."

"Why not?"

"Because I'm not." I locked my door and ran out the building. My heart was broken; I was very hurt and not thinking clearly. I decided to go to the clinic where they give free pregnancy tests. He tagged along right behind me, like a sad puppy.

"Go away, Rell. I can't stand the sight of your lying ass."

He didn't say a word; he just stayed close behind me. I walked into the clinic feeling weak, sick, and annoyed. "Hi, I would like to take a pregnancy test."

"Okay, come this way. I'll be with you shortly," the nurse said. She returned with a small cup and told me to fill it up and bring it back to her. While I was waiting, I didn't know how to feel but angry, because I was dealing with Rell and didn't even know he had a baby. In a way, he was denying his daughter by keeping her a secret.

The nurse came back with a smile on her face. "Are you ready to be a mommy? Because you're pregnant," she said in her West Indian accent.

"Am I really?" I gave off this happy smile but deep inside, I really didn't know what to feel. I was happy, confused, scared, and sad, all at the same time.

"Well, we have great prenatal care inside this clinic," the nurse said.

"Thank you," I said.

"You're welcome and congratulations."

I walked out of the clinic, but Rell was nowhere in sight. All I cared about was keeping this baby safe. I wasn't going to repeat the same drama I went through with Jay. On my way home, I thought about how Jay caused me to lose my baby, and Rell telling me he already had a baby. I was in a daze. I was fucked up mentally. When I got to my building, Rell was sitting on my steps.

"So what's the verdict?" he said.

"What does it matter to you?"

"Are you pregnant?"

"Yes, I am, Rell, and trust me—I'm not having an abortion."

He got up and walked off. I continued up the steps into my building without looking back. "That's right "bounce" bitch my baby, and I don't need you." When I got up stairs, I called Fatima.

"What's up, chica"

"Nothing. I'm just pregnant."

"What?" Tima yelled. "Are you keeping it?"

"Yes."

"What did Rell say?"

"Where do I start? This asshole tells me he has a two-year-old daughter."

"What?"

"Hell, yeah, on top of that, he tells me he ain't having no more kids. I'm keeping my baby—fuck him. I told him to leave me the fuck alone."

"You know he's not going to stay away," Fatima said.

"He's a fucking idiot, and right about now, I don't care what he does."

"We having a baby," Fatima started singing.

"You so stupid, Tima. Now it's time to act like an adult, I have to get me a job."

"You tell your mother yet?"

"Nah, I just found out myself. Telling you I was pregnant made me feel so much better and so much happier about having this baby. Fuck Rell."

"Do what you gotta do, chica."

"You know that's right Tima. It's all about me and this baby. Everything else is secondary. You know how that saying goes: mommy's baby; daddy's maybe."

Tima was my closest cousin besides Shantae; we might as well have been sisters. She was in college, and she got whatever she wanted. She was driving, she was beautiful, and she liked to playing the game with these niggas. As for her, a baby was the last thing on her agenda. I knew I could always count on her. What I liked most about her was she didn't give a fuck about playing them, and she didn't give a fuck if she got caught. She was just like one of the guys; she just was an inner instead of an outer. She had one true love—Alvin—but he was locked up. She always said she wasn't doing any bids with a motherfucker. She was too cute for that, and that bastard would see her when he got out.

It had been a whole month, and I had not heard from Rell. He didn't call me, and I definitely didn't call him or go anywhere near his block, even though I was dying to call him. To be honest, I was missing him.

Damn, I must have been glowing because the men were coming at me hard. I told Debra I was pregnant. I didn't know if she was happy or not, but it didn't matter because I'd decided I was keeping my baby.

I started doing my prenatal care at the clinic. Everything was going well, and I was in my first trimester. Being pregnant was a beautiful thing; I loved it. My hair was growing longer and thicker, and my skin and complexion was fabulous. I wore miniskirts and heels. I was a knock-em-dead pregnant bitch; I was "working it" and working it hard.

Rell must have heard how I looked because out of the blue, I got an unexpected call.

"Hey, Taraine."

"Who is this?" I asked, even though I knew who the fuck it was.

"Stop playing, Tee. You know it's me, Rell."

"Kiss my ass," I said.

"Can I come over to talk to you?"

"No, we don't have anything to talk about Rell. Good bye." Usually, he would have rung my phone one thousand times, but not this time. About an hour later, my bell rang.

"Who is it?"

"It's Rell."

I started jumping up and down. Even though I wanted to hate his tired-ass I still loved him. Before I opened the door, I had to get into my defense mode. "What the fuck you want, Rell?"

He just walked in, grabbed me, and started tonguing me down. "Taraine, I'm sorry," he said as he hugged me tight.

I tried to fight him off but couldn't. He was holding me for dear life. He closed the door and locked it and then walked me to my bedroom. He was kissing me so gently, it felt so good. It seemed like forever since I'd had sex. My body was going through so many changes. "No, stop, we can't do this," I said. My mind was saying no, but my body was saying yes. I wanted him so bad.

He lifted up the tank top I had on and started kissing all over my belly. "You're gonna have my baby Tee?"

"Yes," I said.

He started kissing me gently.

"Rell, you hurt me so bad. Why are you here?"

"I'm sorry, Taraine. I love you. I never meant to hurt you. I was just afraid. I'm sorry for putting my hands on you. I'm sorry, baby." He was saying all this as he kissed and undressed me. I finally let go, and we began having sex and doing everything imaginable and everything unimaginable. I was in my glory; I was in the moment. We laid there for a while, just holding one another. Then it was back to reality.

"Let's talk, Rell. First of all, why didn't you tell me about your daughter?"

"Honestly, I don't know." We started kicking it, and we got real close. "I felt if I told you, you wouldn't want to be with me."

"What's her name?"

"Mone'"

"So are you still with Mone' mother?"

"No, but" … he said.

"But what?"

"We're still close," he said

"Oh, so that means you're still fucking her."

"Nah, we don't rock like that. She got a man, he said."

"Yeah, whatever. I said"

"Now, who told you, you could put your hands on me?"

"I was mad; I thought you were trying to play me. When I saw you talking to Cee, that shit got me tight. He said"

"I lived that life with Jay, Rell—all the fighting, arguing and being out of control."

He yelled, "Don't compare me to the next nigga!"

"I'm not comparing you to him; I'm just letting you know that's not the life I want to live—arguing and fighting over dumb shit. You feel me."

"You right, Tee."

"So are you ready to have this baby growing inside of me, Rell?"

"Yeah, I'm ready, Tee."

"So let's make it happen," I said and kissed him on the cheek. It definitely didn't feel like the last time I got pregnant. This was the one; this was how it was supposed to be. This was how I was supposed to feel.

Chapter 3

He Turned Bitch on Me

I was in my eighth month of pregnancy, and this man was driving me crazy. He was getting on my last damn nerve with his begging. I couldn't take this shit; he was stressing me out. I needed to get away from him, so I decided to leave town for a little while and go to Atlanta to stay with one of my best friends—just to get away, relax, and collect my thoughts. He called my phone constantly, but I refused to answer, and he knew not to call my friend Teensie's phone. Teensie was my best friend; she was older, but we always connected on the same level. She wasn't on no game-playing shit; she gave you a piece of her mind without giving it a second thought.

"Thanks for letting me come down here for a while. I needed to get away from Rell. Yo, that motherfucker is out of control. Every time I turn around, he's begging for money. If he wasn't begging, we were arguing, and if we weren't arguing, we were fucking. I'm so worn out, and I don't want to harm the baby with his foolishness."

"I understand, my doors are always open to you. Look at you, girl. How the fuck are you rocking a cat suit at eight months' pregnant, and that shit looks good on you, too."

"Well, I'm glad you think I look good because at times he had me feeling unattractive and miserable. He smokes weed 24/7, and that shit is a turn-off. Every time I walk out the door, he's on my ass. 'Where you going? Who's gonna be there?' But I'm here, girl, so fuck it; let's leave his ass in Brooklyn. What's up for the night?" I asked.

"Why? What you want to do?"

"I don't know; let's go to a lounge. I want to check out that scene."

"Are you serious?"

"Yes, I'm serious."

Her husband gave her the keys to his Benz, and we were out.

"I'm going to the club," I sang.

"Rell is going to have a fit," Teensie said.

We looked at each other and started laughing.

"Rell who? That mother fucker don't own me. You don't see NO ring on my finger. I just got a baby in the oven, and what that bastard don't know, won't hurt him trust me. 'Cause I'm a bad bitch."

We went to this lounge called the Spot Light. As soon as we walked in, I started doing my two-step. I was open. I knew I ain't had no business being up nobody's lounge, but I was free and just wanted a peace of mind from the bullshit. While I was doing my thing, I heard this whisper in my ear from behind.

"What's up, sexy?"

I turned around, and smiled at this fine-ass-looking piece of specimen, dressed down from head to toe, and he smelled oh, so good. I thought, *Damn, you're sexy as hell.*

"How you doing, sweetness?"

Hearing his deep toned voice had my pussy in an uproar. "I'm good, thank you." Then I thought, *Bitch, snap out of it.*

You're eight months pregnant, but ain't nothing wrong with a little bit of flirting. Teensie and I walked over to the bar so she could order her drink and of course, order me a virgin drink. Then we went to sit and check out the scene. There were a lot of fine-looking men up in here. *Um, I may be changing my location after I have my baby,* I thought.

Why can't Rell be on some laid-back shit. All he worries about is getting high and fucking. I'm starting to question the way I feel about him. Could it be my hormones that have me feeling this way? Or I am so turned off by him, and just ready to say fuck it and kick his ass to the curb.

I know these dudes recognized I was pregnant but they were still trying to hit on me. A couple of them even passed me their number, and I damn sure took them. *Hey, I might want to call them up in a couple of months, because if Rell don't get his shit together, we're done.*

We left the lounge at 1:00 AM. It was a nice, mature spot. I would love to go back, once I have this baby.

My girl Teensie—she is the real deal. She has been through a lot, and she was able to offer me a lot of insight on my situation. She was the type of woman who didn't have to do a lot to get what she wanted. Her husband was very good to her; he was the typical man we all looked for. When I say he treated her like a queen, I mean that literally. Some women get so lucky; the way her husband treated her is how all women should be treated, like a motherfucking queen. *Damn, and here I am with loser number two.*

For the remainder of my time in Atlanta, I just relaxed and did the normal shit with my girl, which was watching movies and shopping at the mall. We also went to the beach; I just did me. The sad part is that these are the things I should have been doing with my baby daddy in Brooklyn. I shouldn't have needed to run away from home. I stayed for two weeks, and then I returned home to get ready for motherhood.

As soon as I got back home, this man was on my ass, wanting sex. My baby was moving like crazy; the last thing I wanted to do was fuck.

"Ma, I missed you," he said, sounding real pitiful.

I thought, *Yeah, whatever.*

"I got some news, baby."

"Oh, yeah, what's that?"

"I got a job," he said proudly.

"Get the fuck out of here. Not you."

"Yeah, babe, everything's going to be just fine. Our baby is going to be good."

"Whatever you say, Rell." *When I see him going to work, that's when I'll believe it.*

He did start working—for about a week before his ass quit, claiming they were making a slave out of him. After that, all we did was argue all the time. I couldn't stand looking at him. He made me sick to my stomach.

<><><>

My family tried to give me a surprise baby shower, but my little cousin gave it away. When I walked into the party, I said, "Surprise, I already knew." They were mad as hell at whoever gave it away. It was all love; I was still happy. I received so many gifts; I wouldn't have to buy too much of anything for a while. Rell didn't even show up, but he wasn't missed at all. Most of my family could see right through his ass. They saw him for the jerk he was. They just dealt with him because I was with him. I was blind-sided by him—or was I? No, I wasn't. I just wanted my child to have a father.

I went for my last prenatal checkup, and the doctor didn't like the sound of the baby's heartbeat. He sent me over to the main hospital to be admitted. The doctor came to me and told me they were going to induce my labor. I later found out that induced labor caused more pain than natural labor. Rell finally arrived at the hospital; by then the pain was so unbearable and I was yelling, screaming and cursing his ass out. I was all drugged up and talking out my head.

Why did you do this to me? Why did you do this, you dumb ass?" I remember him coming to me and saying he'd be right back. He never returned, and I was in too much pain to care. I just wanted this baby out of me. My mother came and held me down, but at some point, she got fed up with me and my silly talk. I kept calling Rell's name and cursing his ass out. All I remember is my mother saying, "He ain't here," in a nasty tone—in other words, stop worrying about that asshole and focus on having this baby. Even though I was in pain, I understood exactly where she was coming from.

At one point I was on my knees in the hospital bed, and the nurse came in yelling, "No, my dear, you cannot be on your knees like that!" Thirty-five hours had passed, and the pain didn't ease up at all. I tried to get up to go to the bathroom and started yelling for a nurse. I felt like I had to shit.

The nurse came to check me. "Wait," she said, "don't push. Let me get the doctor. I see the baby's head."

"No, I have to use the bathroom." I was feeling like I was constipated, and I just needed to push it out.

The nurse continued to yell, "No, Mommy that is the baby!"

This made me so frustrated, because I knew how I felt at that moment. I didn't give a damn about what this lady was talking about. I knew what I had to do; I just started talking to myself. "Okay, bitch, it is time to push."

The doctor said, "Press your chin down into your chest, take a deep breath, and push."

As I was doing what the doctor said, I wondered how the fuck could I be comfortable with a thousand people looking all up my ass. I pushed, then paused; pushed, then paused.

The doctor said "Okay, you're looking good. Let's try to push a couple more times." I pushed a couple more time; then I felt the baby slide right out of me. "It's a girl," the doctor said, all happy. You would have thought he was the damn father.

I was so happy but so damn tired, all I wanted to do was hold her, and then go to sleep. My mother came to me and said, "You thought that was hard. That was the easy part."

I looked at her like; *you're just joking, right?* I'm glad my mother was there, because I passed the hell out until they woke me up to feed the baby. I still didn't have a name for her, but I knew it had to be beautiful and different. I had to hold it down because once again, Rell turned bitch on me. My baby was so beautiful and the name that came to mind was Nicera. I don't know where the name came from, but I liked it. She had a caramel complexion with curly jet-black hair. She looked just like me, as if I just created her all on my own. I was happy and in love with my little girl, my little Cee-Cee.

Rell came strolling in my hospital room, and I didn't even give him a second look. "I'm sorry I left, Tee. I don't know what happened. I saw you in so much pain and got scared. I bugged out and left," he said, sounding like a straight up bitch.

"Oh, so I guess you just up and left when your other daughter was born, too, huh?"

"I wasn't even in town when she had the baby."

I just laid there, looking at the jackass I chose to have a baby by. I couldn't hold it in any longer. I had to let out what I was truly feeling. "It's time for you to grow the fuck up Rell but you know what, I'm not going to let you steal my joy right now. I decided to cut out conversation short because I felt the anger piling up and it ain't even about him right now it's about my little princess.

Good thing I got myself together because before I knew it everybody was coming to the hospital to see my little princess, and I didn't want them to see how angry I was with Rell.

My mother convinced me to breast-feed her. I didn't like it — it hurt like hell — but it was so much better at night and it was also a way for us to bond. I love the fact of not getting up throughout the night to heat up bottles. It was all about me and my baby for right now. Rell could kiss my ass; he was just extra baggage. Even though I'd just had Nicera, I knew I had to get up and get shit back in order. I needed to go to work or school.

Before I knew it, I was doing both—working and going to college. It was hard as hell, but it had to be done. Rell didn't like the simple fact that I had my shit together and that I was doing it, so he worked his way back to his first daughter's mother. At first, I didn't believe it, but after a while, the proof was in the pudding. I didn't care. I was still doing him whenever I wanted too. The sex wasn't even good anymore, not that it was that great to begin with. I just wasn't ready to go out there and share my va-jay-jay with anyone else, so I decided to stick with what I knew until I was ready for something new.

Me and Vanessa, his other daughter's mother, would get into it constantly, until we finally bumped heads near my college, and I put a beating on that ass. This bitch tried to step to me like she was hardcore. She was in the streets, yelling, "Bitch, you don't know me, I will fuck your ass up." I passed Rell my bag and it was on.

"I don't need to know you, bitch, but what I do know is Rell and I was fucking the shit out of each other this morning, and that's all you need to know." I yelled as I pulled my razor out my mouth and slashed her right across her face. As she reached for her face, I went in and beat that bitch's ass. Rell was trying to pull us apart, but I was too enraged, he couldn't stop me I was out of control. A couple of people managed to pull us apart, as Rell yelled, "Come on, Ma, they called the cops." I turned to him and started breaking on him. "Shut the fuck up before I cut your dumb ass." I continued about my business like nothing ever happened. Nobody saw me cut that bitch, just Rell, and that motherfucker had better not say shit. Before I could get to my college building, a cop car pulled up to the curb. They jumped out on me like I just shot somebody.

"Could you step over here for a minute, miss?"

"For what?" I said.

They walked up on me, turned me around, and placed the handcuffs on me, as they read me my rights.

They took Vanessa's ass to the hospital and took me to the Seventy-ninth Precinct. While I was waiting, this dumb-ass black cop asked me a bunch of ignorant ass questions, but I didn't hear him—fuck that. I was ready to beat that bitch ass again, just for the simple fact of me being here.

Two hours passed, and I was still in this fucking precinct, still in the same spot. I looked up and watch them escort this crazy bitch inside the precinct; they had her ass in handcuffs and her face was bandaged up. I looked her dead in her face, and I yelled, "Bring it, bitch!"

"Ms. Davis, if you don't shut up, I'm going to cuff you to the chair."

"Ms. Johnson, are you pressing charges?" the cop asked.

I jumped in. "If she's pressing charges, then so am I." I looked at that bitch like, *You better so"NO".*

She said, "No, sir."

He looked at her as if she was crazy. "Are you pressing charges, Ms. Davis?"

"No."

I'm so surprised they didn't lock my ass up. I took it as a message to get my shit together. He gave both of us papers to appear in court before a judge. They let me go first and warned me not to stay in the surrounding area or they would lock my ass up for trespassing.

I went to get my baby from my grandmother Flo's house. She watched Nicera while I went to school, and my mother watched her while I went to work.

"Where you been?" my grandmother asked.

I didn't want to go into full details with her, so I told her I had to stay late at school.

Mommy," Nicera said, as she ran towards me.

"How's Mommy baby? I love you." As I got her dressed, I was thinking, *your father is a piece of shit, but I'll get that motherfucker.* I had to rush home so I could get ready for work. It was hard, trying to be a mother, go to school, go to work and then a mother again, but it had to be done. When I got to my door, who was standing there? Rell.

"You're out of control, Ma."

"No, your bitch is out of control. This shit is all your fault, anyway. I'm tired of dealing with your dumb shit, Rell. It's not worth it, you're not worth it."

"Oh, now I ain't worth it," he said.

"The games — definitely not. You need to grow the fuck up and get you mind on the right track. The 'I need to be a real man track and the - I need to be a father to my child track'. I have one baby, Rell. I don't need two. You want to be with Vanessa? Go right ahead, but leave me the fuck alone."

"You don't understand, Ma. She is threatening to take my daughter away from me."

"Whatever you say, Rell. I'm not going there with you. You wanted to play this back-and-forth game, and I went with it for a while. Yeah, I fucked you, but notice it was only when I wanted it. Now she wants to play like she's Teflon, and threaten me over the phone and unfortunately for her she got caught in her own fucking web. I'll see her ass in court, and she better come correct."

"Please, baby, don't do this to me!" he shouted.

"Don't do what to you, Rell? I'm so fucking tired of your lying ass crying when I tell you I'm done — it's pathetic. I'm not going through this bullshit any longer."

Then Nicera started crying. "Look, I'm going to lay her down. I need to get at least an hour of sleep before I go to work." As I began dozing off Rell comes behind me like a sad puppy dog, as usual. "I'm sorry, Taraine. I don't know what's wrong with me." And that was the last thing I heard him say before I dozed off. I got up, tired as hell, but I needed to go to work. I knew I couldn't depend on his tired ass to help me pay my bills. If I depended on him, Nicera and I would be starving and homeless.

Chapter 4

See Da Real from Da Fake

"Oh, shit!" I shouted as I popped up from a deep sleep. It was a quarter to nine. I was supposed to be in court at 9:00 AM. *Damn!*

The phone rang. "Yo, are you ready?"

"Rell, I just woke up. Are you still going with me, or are you going to stay with Nicera?"

"I'm going with you."

"All right. I'll take her to my mother's house."

We got to the court building around 10:30 but they hadn't called me yet. I didn't see that bitch nowhere in sight.

They called both of our names. I stepped up toward the judge. They called her name again: "Vanessa Johnson." Still, no response. The judge continued preaching on and on to me about society, the violence, this and that. He called her name once more and there was still no answer, so he dismissed the case but not before telling me he had better not see my ass in his courtroom again.

After we left the court building, we went to get something to eat and to have the same old tired-ass talk.

"Rell, seriously this shit has to stop. I can't afford to do no time because you're playing this back-and-forth game between me and Vanessa. It has gotten way out of control. What do you want, Rell?"

"You know I want you, Ma. I want you; I want to be with you."

This little motherfucker was lying through his teeth, but I gave him the benefit of the doubt. I believed Rell loved his daughter to death, and she was looking more and more like him but in a cute way. "I think you should get yourself together, move in, and try to help me out a little."

He looked at me with a smile. "Are you for real? Do you want me to move in?"

"I want you to be a man and a great father. Put your best foot forward, and try to help me out. I can't make you be a man. You have to do that on your own. Are you ready to do the right thing, Rell?"

"No doubt."

"Okay, let's give it a try. We'll see what happens."

<><><>

He started moving all his shit back in. At first, everything was all good; then I started to feel like I had two babies instead of one once again. There was a tug of war going on with my breast. Rell wasn't the help I thought he would be. He was still on the same bullshit, but it was more noticeable now. He was an arrogant weed-head motherfucker. Every time I turned around, this chick was calling my house and hanging up. I guess that bitch was looking for a buck-fifty on the other side of her face. "Rell, you need to tell that lunatic to stop calling my house and hanging up. I know it's her dumb ass."

"I ain't got to tell her shit. You tell her."

"Why? You don't have enough balls to tell her."

"Ma, I'm not going there with you."

I started yelling at his ass, "If you would have put that bitch in her place to begin with, we wouldn't be going through this shit."

"Taraine, you have to realize I have a child with her."

"I understand that, but I told you before you came here that I didn't want NO bullshit from you."

He just ignored me. "Yo, let me get twenty dollars."

"No, go ask that bitch for twenty dollars. Any money I have is going toward milk and Pampers. You're in here acting like your ass is on some other type of drug. Let me find out you're out there sniffing coke."

He started begging me for the money. I just looked at his ass like he was crazy. "You need to take a break from the weed and get your mind right. You are losing it, Rell."

"Do I tell you what to take a break from?"

"No, but do I go around begging you for money? Hell no."

He must have been lacing his weed because he was totally out of control. Nicera started crying, so I went to tend to her. I finally got her to go back to sleep, and when I walked back into my living room; I realized this asshole had left. I looked on the couch at my bag, which was open. I checked my bag and realized he got me for a hundred dollars. "Is this man on crack or what?" I was so heated; I didn't know what to do. I already knew what was going to go down when this man decided to return home.

Four hours passed, and he was a no-show. I put the latch on the door and went to bed. By sunrise the thief still hadn't came home. I was more than livid now—shit, I was ready to fight. I looked at Nicera sleeping, and her beauty calmed me down. She looked so peaceful; she had no clue what type of father she had. I managed to doze off again but was awakened by Rell trying to get in, but he couldn't because I'd put the safety lock on. I got up and closed my bedroom door so he wouldn't wake the baby and took my ass back to sleep. Now, he'd get in when I fucking opened the door, damn cokehead.

As long as Nicera slept, I slept. I was so glad I didn't have any classes today, but I had to be at work by seven o'clock that evening. I didn't know if I was going to go, because he'd definitely be able to get in, and I might come home to an empty apartment.

What was going on with him? They say you really get to know a person when you move in with him but this was beyond crazy. I was definitely not feeling this shit. I was ready to throw all his property out; this was not what I'd asked for. This was not a happy home and this was another sign for me to leave his ass alone. But did I follow my gut instinct? Of course I didn't.

I never got my hundred dollars back, either, just like I never got back the fifty dollars he'd borrowed from me when we first met. It's so sad but the signs were always in my face and I chose to ignore them. Sometimes you reap what you sow and I was feeling it in every way imaginable.

Chapter 5

Raise Up or Raise Out

As I laid in my bed, I thought, all I ever wanted was a good man—a real man, someone to connect with, someone who was on my level. I turned over and looked at this dumb motherfucker, my baby daddy. I wasn't one for putting a brother down, but I was just fed up with this shit. I knew how it felt to hit rock bottom. He had to raise up or raise the fuck out. All he wanted to do was smoke weed and get his dick sucked. He had no finesse about him, no sex appeal, nothing. I loved Rell, but he was never going to change. I didn't even see any father/daughter connection with him and Nicera.

Could a man be jealous of his own child? Could he be that ignorant? I didn't know but it was killing me to think about it.

That night I took Nicera over to my mother's for the weekend. I needed to get away from this man once again. Fatima was having a venting session at her house. I used to be against these bitch sessions, but as I got older, I realized it was definitely good for me to attend them every now and then. When I got there, Kelly, Shantae, and Slim was there.

"What's up y'all?"

"Hey, where's the baby?" Kelly asked.

"She's with Debra."

We all sat in the living room, eating, drinking, and getting comfortable. Monica, who we liked to call Slim, just came out of nowhere, saying, "Why the fuck can't I get Ron to give me head? He acts as if he scared to taste this pussy." We all started laughing.

"Y'all laughing, but I'm serious. He's so quick to put his uncircumcised dick in my face."

"Uncircumcised?" I said, looking disgusted at the thought. "And you like giving him head with all that extra skin?"

"Well, I had to get used to it, but I get the job done."

"That's not sanitary," Kelly said.

"He must think I can get my shit off with him just being inside of me."

"Oh, hell, no," Fatima said. "Is that man crazy? Fuck that—if I'm giving you head, you better believe your ass is going down on me. He had better eat my pussy like it was steak and lobster dinner. I don't give a fuck if he is full from a five-course meal. His ass better make room."

"You know what the problem is?" Shantae said. "A lot of guys don't know how to eat pussy. They think licking up and down is going to get the job done. They don't even realize how much power the clit has."

"Well, my problem is deeper than sex right now; I am so turned off by Rell. I mean, I literally can't stand this man anymore. I just want him out of my life. He's not going to change. I realize that now, and it's not my job to change him. I'm supposed to be his women, his quote/unquote "wifey," not his mother or his fucking babysitter. He steals from me, and he's no help with Nicera at all. We're definitely not on the same level. We never were, and I don't know what to do. Sometimes I want to tell him to get the fuck out, and then there's times when I feel maybe he'll get his shit together. Maybe he'll wake up and make a change. I think I'm yearning for the perfect relationship or the perfect man, when I know, deep down inside, that I'm not going to get that from him. He has a lot of growing up to do. He needs to stop trying to impress his so called street friends and try to impress me. To be honest, I'm so confused, and I really don't know what to do. I never was the type of woman to cheat on my man but why not? He's been doing that shit to me."

They all looked at me like, *What?*

"Yeah, that's why I was arrested, because I beat that bitch ass, and I cut her across her face."

"Who?" Fatima said.

"His baby mother—that stupid bitch. I tried to take her fucking face off, and that wasn't right, but between him going back and forth, it got crazy. I knew eventually I would see her, and I was prepared. We went to court, and she didn't show up, so the case was dismissed. His dumb ass was there when all this shit went down."

"Get the fuck out of here," Kelly said.

"Yup, that mother fucker was playing both of us, and I didn't want to get into a relationship with anybody else, so I just settled for his bullshit. That bitch was on my last nerve with her mouth, and once I saw her, I lost my mind. I should have let her have his dumb ass, because what I'm going through now ain't worth it."

"You know what the problem is?" Fatima said, with her hands on her hips. "Y'all fall too motherfucking hard for these niggas, instead of taking these bastards for what they're worth. Fuck that—I'm not falling hard for anybody unless he had a lot to offer. Don't come to me with your fucking baggage. Once you found out he already had a child and he was scared to tell you that was your cue to get the fuck out of dodge. As for you, Slim, once he didn't go diving into your pussy, I wouldn't have even blown on his dick. Play the game with these motherfuckers like they play the game with us. Eventually, you'll be able to see the real from the fake. Until then, fuck 'em."

We sat there looking at her, like, "Preach, bitch."

Fatima is right, I thought on my way home, *but I'm not that type of woman.* On the other hand, I'd made too many sacrifices for this man. I dumbed out too many times. I didn't want to live the life that Fatima lived; all I wanted was the family life. I always wanted to be the wife with the house and the kids. Now I was on my way home to half a man, a man with so much potential but showed me "it is what it is," in other words, take me as I am or leave me the fuck alone.

<><><>

When I got home, he was nowhere in sight. *Good,* I thought. I decided to take a nice bubble bath, listen to some R & B, and relax my mind, body, and soul. It felt so good, venting at Fatima's. It seemed like I got so much off my chest.

Around 3:30 AM, I heard the key unlocking the door. That used to be one of our rules—never let sun hit us. This meant to be home before sunrise. He surely let the sun catch him the night he stole my money out of my bag. He came sliding into bed. His ignorant ass probably didn't realize Nicera wasn't in her crib—probably didn't care. I felt his dick getting hard as he rubbed up against my ass. I was so horny, but fuck that—my shit was on lock.

"Rell, you're not fucking me," I said in a nonchalant manner.

"What?"

"You heard me; this pussy right here is closed for business."

"We need to talk." I said as I turned to him so I could look into his eyes.

"Why are you here?"

"What's your purpose?"

"Neither one of us is getting any younger. We have a child together that you barely pay any attention to. You're not pulling your weight around here. All you do is take, take, take, and you're draining me. Every time you get a job, you quit."

"What are your priorities Rell?"

"Do you think the street is where it's at? Because eventually, playing the corner runs out. When I met you the corner was never your thing. You were there for a minute, and then you were gone. You keep playing the corner, and you're going to end up dead or in jail. Look at your brother—he's in jail for life." His brother Dwayne looked just like him; they could pass for twins. He let the streets get him at an early age. "You have two little girls to live for. That nickel-and-dime bullshit you chasing on the streets need to stop and you need to find a job. Do you value what you have here?"

"Yes, I do, Taraine."

"Well, when are you going to make a change? Because, this right here is not working. We should be living it up; it should be strictly about family. If you want to be with the drama queen, Vanessa, then do that. Just stop wasting my fucking time. If you want these broads in the street, then once again, stop wasting my time. I'm about making it happen. I got goals, and I don't have time to play these games." I knew it was going in one ear and out the other, but I was trying to give it one last try before I decided to let it all hang out.

"I give you my word, Taraine, I'm going to change. No more bull shitting in the streets. I'm going to get a job and take care of my family; you'll see," he said, as he started kissing me on my lips.

I pushed him off me. "Don't think I forgot about my money you took out my bag. That's some cracked-head bullshit you did." He started laughing. "I'm not playing, you better triple my shit by tomorrow."

"See, Ma, you just told me to stop being in the streets, and now you're telling me to triple it."

"I just want back what you took from me. You knew how to take it right; then you should know how to replace it with interest." Then, of course, I had to give in. Damn, I know they say pussy is a powerful thing, but dick is, too, especially when

you're horny as hell. Rell put in extra work tonight …
mmmm.hmmmm.

He got up and cooked breakfast—that's one thing I can say
about him; he had skills in the kitchen. We talked some more,
and then he left, and I went back to sleep. I was going to give
this shit one last try, just for Nicera's sake, but if don't get his
act together; I was saying fuck it to everything.

Chapter 6

Surprise

Everything was going good with Rell and I; he found another job working for FedEx. He even tried to cut down on the weed, but of course, that didn't last for too long. I guess I was asking for a miracle with that. Nicera was turning a year old, and we were getting ready for her party. I always wondered why people gave parties for one-year-olds but bought a lot of shit for adults. We had everything, and none of it was for her — all types of food, liquor, and of course, loud music. This was a party for adults; there were more adults there than kids. Everybody got drunk, talked shit, danced, spilled shit, etc. Even though Nicera didn't know what the hell was going on, the party still turned out nice. She received plenty of gifts. Rell was videotaping the party, but his ass was so drunk and he ended up recording the ceiling and the walls. That was okay. I guess it was the thought that count. Well, he did get the best part of the party, which was my grandmother and grandfather doing their same old two-step that never got old; it just got more significant with time. What they had is what I wanted with Rell. Throughout all their ups and downs, they did whatever it took to make it work. She was his everything, and he was hers. They took care of home together. To me, it seemed like they were inseparable; they were together for over forty years and still going strong.

I wanted that type of relationship—when someone would see Taraine, they'd see Jorrell, and vice versa. I know he wanted it, but I didn't know if he was mature enough to see it was not about what his boys thought; and that it was about having a family and making it happen by all means necessary.

We got on the grind of trying to strengthen our relationship. We were happy and in love ... until the day of my surprise party—damn.

<><><>

Fatima and the girls decided to give me a surprise party— nothing too big; a couple of my girls showed up. It was more like a dinner party. I was enjoying myself, as usual, talking, eating, and drinking. Fatima's doorbell rang.

"I got it!" I yelled.

"Sit your ass down; I got it," Fatima said, rushing to the door.

I looked at her. "Okay, bitch, it ain't that serious. It's your door. You can open it anytime you want." As I walked back to the living room, I felt someone all on my ass. I turned around to see this man dressed in all black from head to toe. He reached around me and placed a blindfold over my eyes, and then he started dancing all on me from behind. All I could do was smile and giggle in shock, like a teenage girl being humped on by her little teenage boyfriend. He started grinding all on me, and I thought, *this ain't no teenage shit here.* He took me by the hand and sat me in the chair. I didn't know what I was getting myself into—or should I say, what Fatima was getting me into. He started directing my hand in all types of places. All I heard was the other girls oohing and aahing. What I knew for sure was whatever I was touching had me very excited. The next thing I knew, he took the blindfold off, and I was very turned on by what I saw. Standing in front of me was my chocolate delight—he was fine as hell. *Damn!* He made Rell look like Batman's sidekick, Boy Wonder.

"I was told you're the birthday girl," he said.

"Hell, yeah," I said. I began squirming in my chair as I looked him up and down from head to toe. I got to his midsection and then went a little further. Oh my *God*—this man was packing. I looked at Fatima, smiled, and winked, like, *Bitch, do you see all this standing in front of me?* She must have known what I was thinking.

"Is it all his, girl?" she asked with a curious-looking smile on her face. I found myself sliding my hands down his jock strap. "Hell, yeah!" I shouted, and he was hard as hell. Next thing I knew, he picked me up and he laid me on the floor. He had me all wet between the thighs as he continued putting all his freaky moves on me. I never cheated on Rell, but the attraction going on between us right now was telling a different story. I wanted him to peel my panties off and take me, right here right now. He started grinding on me and all I could feel was his manhood thrusting against my clit. I could not believe this was happening. I felt myself catching an orgasm right there in the middle of Fatima's living room floor, without any penetration. There was definitely something going on between us, even if it was just for that moment. All of a sudden, he started tonguing me down as if we were alone. Even the smell of his minty breath turned me on.

"What's your name, beautiful?" he whispered in a seductive tone.

"Taraine," I said, giving it back to him in my on seductive way.

"Can I have you tonight?"

I was thinking, *Hell, no,* but the way he had me cumin without being deep in me, I wanted to say, "Hell, yeah," but I did not respond to that.

He got up and helped me off the floor. I guess he forgot he had a job to do and that he was there to make money. He started interacting with the other ladies. They were also enjoying him, but not as much as I did.

Fatima got all excited. She yelled, "Pull your money out, ladies!" He was flipping them, stroking them; he was doing it all, but he did not give any of them the treatment I got. All I was thinking about was how good of a fuck he would be. Should I feel bad for feeling this way? I didn't. I did not have one guilty feeling about wanting to fuck another man.

His time was up. He said his good-byes and was ready to leave; he turned to me and asked, "How long are you going to be here? I would like to take you out."

"Really," I said. "Is that what you do at every party? Take a female out after?"

"Nah, but there's something about you. I know you felt it just as much as I did."

"Yes, I did, but I don't know you. You could be some type of serial rapist or murderer," I said.

"That's true, beautiful, but trust me, I'm not. Let me take you out, so you can get to know me on a different level, outside of what you just saw."

"I don't even know your name—well, Black Stallion, but that's your stripper name. Who's the real man outside of this getup?"

He said, "My name is LaQuan. So is it on, beautiful? Can I spend a little money on you? Can you spare a little bit of your time on someone like me?"

I gave in and said yes. "You can pick me up here in another two hours." I gave him my cell number and told him to call me when he was on his way.

I went back inside with my girls, and we continued enjoying the rest of the night. I didn't dare tell them I was meeting him in a couple of hours, even though I knew Tima would have loved to hear that. I was sitting on the couch, thinking about how Rell and I had just gotten back on the right track, so what the fuck was I doing? I totally contradicted myself with all the shit I claimed I wanted. Well, it was only a little fun. *There's no harm in it, as long as I don't step out of line.* The time was getting closer, and I was feeling all queasy inside, due to the fact I was about to do something I had never done before. Next thing I knew, my phone was ringing.

"Hey, beautiful, I'm on my way. It's going to take me about fifteen minutes to get there."

"That's cool. I'll be downstairs." I started wrapping it up with the girls. "That was fun, ladies, but I think it's time for me to get my black ass home. Thank you, bitches, for everything. I love y'all. Tima, where you get that stripper from?" I said as I winked my eye at her, good choice.

"Yeah, bitch, you know I know how to pick 'em. He's cool; he hangs with Charles. That's why I played the back. It was all for you, girl. You deserve some love and attention." We looked at each other and started laughing. She didn't know I was going to get some more attention. I guess I was just being greedy.

"Tell me the truth, chica—was all that real or was his shit stuffed?"

"Oh, it was definitely all real, hard, and pure as platinum. I wish I could have got a taste of that," I said.

She looked at me in shock. "No, you did not just-say- that, but on the real, y'all were acting as if y'all were in a hotel getting ready to get it on."

I started laughing. "You're so stupid." I knew damn well I was getting ready to go downstairs to meet him. "Well, let me get out of here. I am going to leave Nicera with Debra tonight. This little session tired my ass out. Bye, bitches. I'll call y'all later. I hate to leave, but it's time for me to make my grand exit. Smooches."

When I got downstairs, he was already there. He was driving a cream BMW with beige leather interior. His car was just as fine as he was.

"Hey, beautiful," he said as I got in his car.

I said hi, shyly. "So what do I call you? Black Stallion or LaQuan?"

"You can call me whatever you like, just as long as you mean it."

I started smiling.

He took me to a nice Italian restaurant. I wasn't hungry—at least not for no spaghetti or linguini—but if he wanted to spend his money, I'll let him do just that. I was more than worth it. We ordered our food, and he ordered a bottle of red wine to keep the mood nice and sexy, but he said he would rather have had Dom Perignon—that was his favorite drink. I'm not too much of a drinker, but like I said, he was spending, so I was drinking. Even in regular clothes, he was a sight for sore eyes—*damn!*

"Talk to me, beautiful," he said.

"What you want to know?"

"I want to get to know all about you."

"Let's cut to the chase. You want to fuck me?" I asked.

"Honestly, yeah, I do. I think you're sexy, and you definitely turn me on, so I'm not going to lie. I want you real bad, but I do want to get to know you better."

"Okay, well, as you already know, my name is Taraine. I have a year-old daughter named Nicera. I'm in a relationship with her father."

He stopped me dead in my tracks and said, "No, you were in a relationship with your daughter's father, but I'm about to change all that."

I started smiling. "You think so?" I asked.

"Trust me, beautiful, I know so."

The way he was talking to me turned me on in the worst way. I'd never been attracted to any man the way I was at that moment, but maybe it was just infatuation.

"Okay, enough about me. Tell me a little about you, and don't just tell me all the good shit."

"I'm from the Bx., and I've been doing parties for a little over two years."

I interrupted him. "Oh, so you've been picking up bitches from parties for about two years now?"

"No," he said quickly, "I was in a serious relationship for four years, but about a year after I started doing this job, she couldn't take it anymore. It was too much for her to handle, so we went our separate ways. I was trying to be a sponge and absorb everything about the business. I was a hustler in that sense. I love money, and I love nice things. Believe me, I treated her good, but because I was working extra hard, she took it as neglect. Now, I'm doing this shit my way, on my own time and terms, because I learned the business and how it works for me. She didn't have the patience unless I was spending the money on her. So now, I'm looking for a real woman one who is down for me, just like I'll be down for her." Before I could say another word to him, he reached over and kissed me ever so gently. I could feel my pussy twirling and juicing up all over again. "You smell so good," he said. "Where have you been hiding?"

"One: I don't hang out too much; and two: I never go to strip clubs. You were absolutely a surprise for me from my girl Fatima."

"Well, thank you, Fatima," he said.

We ate and drank a little more. Then he asked me if I wanted to go back to his place.

Hell, yeah—that's what I wanted to say. "I can't, LaQuan. I have to get home."

"Please," he begged, "just for a little while. I promise when you are ready to go, I'll take you home."

"All right," I said, "but remember, you said when I'm ready to go home, right?" I said with a smile.

"Yes, beautiful."

So we got back to his place. It was nice—very nice. You could definitely tell he was into living good. "This is nice," I said, going straight to his couch. "How many bedrooms do you have?"

"Two. I turned one into a gym."

"That was smart. I see why your body is so tight."

He sat on the couch next to me, and we just started talking about random shit, knowing deep inside what both of us wanted to do.

"So what's your favorite movie of all time?" he asked.

"Well I have two. My first one is *New Jack City*—Nino Brown—and the other one is *The Last Dragon*—Bruce Leroy. I don't care how it gets; I could watch those two movies over and over again."

"I got them," he said.

"Stop playing."

He pulled them out and popped *The Last Dragon* in the DVD player. "Would you like something to drink?"

"No, I'm good."

So we started watching *The Last Dragon*, Bruce Leroy looked so damn good in that movie. *He could definitely get it,* I thought. Then I glimpsed at LaQuan and thought, *Damn, you are just as fine, and you can get it, too – right here, right now.*

He leaned toward me as if he knew exactly what I was thinking and started tonguing me down. I was not expecting that—nah, yes I was. His tongue felt so good. He started caressing my breast. He pulled me on top of him in straddle position.

"Beautiful, can you teach me some moves?"

I started laughing because that's what Bruce Leroy said to the woman in the movie. I said, "I could teach you some moves right here in this living room."

So ask me how I ended up in his bedroom. He laid me on his bed and pulled off my shoes. "You think I brought you here to fuck you, right? Well, I'm going to show you different."

No, you can fuck me, I thought, but he got up and pulled a T-shirt out of his dresser drawer.

"You can get comfortable," he said. "I just want to enjoy your company. I want to get to know you, but if you really want to go home, I will take you."

I found myself getting up, not to put my shoes back on but to go take a shower. After my shower, I made a couple of phone calls, one being my mother. I had to let her know I wasn't going home, and if Rell decided to call, I asked her to tell him I was asleep. I called Tima to let her know if Rell called, she shouldn't answer. She was getting ready to ask a thousand and one questions, so I had to cut her ass short. "Just do it, girl. I'll call you later." I hung up; I didn't even give her a chance to say bye. I went back into LaQuan's room and realized he had dozed off, so I tried to climb gently beside him which didn't work because he woke up with a smile on his face.

"Hey, beautiful, you took a while. Get relaxed. Let me go take a shower."

As I got comfortable in his bed waiting for him to return, I thought, *what the fuck are you doing?*

The comforter and the pillows on his bed smelled so good, just like him. It took me back to what went down between us at that party. Right then and there, I could feel myself juicing up. *Stop it, girl. Your nasty ass is out of control. Remember, we're just trying to get to know each other. Nah, I need to be honest with myself. I want to fuck him badly.*

He came out the shower, glistening from head to toe. *Oh, damn, he's trying to take me there. I want this man, bad.* I begin biting gently on my bottom lip; I pulled the covers over my face so he couldn't see how bad I wanted him. He put on some boxers and climbed under the comforter right beside me. We talked and talked until eventually, we fell asleep.

The light from the sun woke me up. He had his arms wrapped around me. I got up and went to the bathroom to rinse my mouth out. When I walked back to the bedroom, I realized I'd broken the number one rule, which was *"never let the sunlight catch us in the streets"* oh well. I looked down at LaQuan, sleeping, and thought, *damn, even in your sleep, you are gorgeous. Well, bitch, the sun is up, so expect a big fight with Rell tonight.*

I lifted the covers and found myself going down on LaQuan. Even while sleeping his pipe was still enormous, the touch of my tongue woke him up real fast. LaQuan started moaning, "Oh, damn, beautiful, what are you doing?" Once he asked that, I started to go in deep on him. I wanted to take him there, so I begin licking on his thighs; then I took it to his balls.

"Oh, beautiful, you're doing your thing, baby."

Got 'em, I thought. I watched him in full pleasure as I twirled his balls all around in my mouth. I was licking and sucking on them like they were my favorite flavored lollipop.

"Beautiful, you're trying to get me open." He pulled me up on top of him. He kissed me and then laid me next to him. He just gazed at me and started running his fingers through my hair. He began kissing me on my lips, then down to my neck, and then finally my "Phatty" — that is what I called her because she's was so thick and pretty. He kissed her so gently, licking her and sucking her in all the right spots. I moaned so hard; it felt so good. I grabbed his head and rotated it in circles. He was feasting on Phatty, he had me ready to scream "I love you!" I could feel my body began to surrender, I could no longer hold on as the feeling began to intensify. I soon found myself having back to back orgasms. I'd never felt like this with Rell ever. I begin to arch my back and moan to this sensational feeling I was experiencing. "Oh, shit, baby."

He said, "Call me Daddy."

"Oh, shit, Daddy, oh, damn." I couldn't even move. He slowly climbed on top of me and began sucking on my breast. He was sucking on my nipples so seductively. I reached down and grabbed his manhood. I realized it had a curve to it. That turned me on even more. I was so anxious to feel him inside of me. He must have known what I was thinking because he looked at me, kissed me, and said, "Relax. I won't hurt you. I promise."

Next thing I knew, he was guiding his dick inside of me. It hurt so bad, but it felt so good as he stroked me nice and slow. When I tried to please him in return, he said, "Beautiful, let me take you there. Let me do my thing. Let me show you what love making is all about." All I could do was wrap my legs around him and enjoy the moment. He had my body shaking uncontrollably, but I couldn't go out like that. He needed to see what I was working with. I got on top of him and gave him the ride of his life. I was whining and grinding all on him, using my muscles to choke his hard pipe. He was moaning, oohing, and aahing out of control. "No, beautiful, don't do that." The next thing I knew, we were both cumming together. All I could do was lie on top of him and calm the savage beast. I didn't want to move; it was so good and I didn't want it to end.

"Damn, that was good," I said.

"It's only the beginning, Taraine." That was the first time he'd called me by my first name since meeting him. "Are you ready for me to take you home, or can you spend the day with me?"

I looked at him and said, "I would love to spend the day with you." I mumbled under my breath, "and the night, too." The Black Stallion rocked my world and I'm not ashamed to say that I fucked him on the first night.

He got up and went into the kitchen to make us some breakfast. I put on his T-shirt and went to help him. When I walked into the kitchen, he said, "take that off," in reference to his T-shirt I was wearing. He walked toward me and pulled it off. I didn't even see the shirt hit the floor before we were fucking again, right on his kitchen sink. He was definitely giving me the fuck of my life.

Is this what I've been missing out on? Or is it that I finally met a man? Even while trying to go hard, he still managed to kiss me as if I was his goddess.

"Oh, Taraine, you feel so good," he said as he stroked phatty hard. I found myself releasing all my unwanted stress right on his sink. He said, "I'm going to make you mine. I'm going to take you away from what's-his-name."

His sex game was tight; it was so right. I can't deny it; I fell in love with this man named LaQuan. *Is it possible?* Everything about him turned me on. I was wide open.

"I thought I was doing the right thing by coming to help you make breakfast, but it looks like we're never going to eat."

"Believe me—I'm going to eat because you taste so good," he said.

"Excuse me—let me go and check on my daughter." I said as I walked away. He smiled as my ass moved in circular motion.

"Hi, Debra, what Nicera doing?"

"Girl, where you at?"

"I'm at a friend house. What is Nicera doing?"

"She's sleeping."

"Did Rell call?"

"Yes, a few times."

"All right. Can you watch Nicera again for me tonight?"

"Yeah, yeah," she said. "Don't be out there getting yourself into no mess."

"I'm not, Deb. I'll call you back." I walked back into the kitchen and watched LaQuan fix my plate. He made beef sausages, eggs, and grits with cheese. "Damn, baby, you can cook, too. You are definitely a keeper."

"Yeah, beautiful, I get busy."

"Oh, yeah! Well, I definitely love a man who can cook—or at least try."

"You are going to like a lot of things about me, not just my sex game." He looked back at me and smiled. Before we finished breakfast, we were going at it again right on his kitchen table. Afterwards, we jumped in his bed and watched a little television, talked about miscellaneous shit, and fucked some more.

This man was exploring me in every way Rell didn't. I was flipped, picked up, tossed up, and backed up in every way possible. I finally fell asleep after that big workout; he had drained my ass out.

I woke up and looked at the clock; it was 3:30 PM. I turned over, and LaQuan wasn't there. This gave me a moment to come back to reality. *Oh, my God! Rell is going to kill me. I am not going home tonight; I can't. I know it will probably make things worse, but I just wanted to let all that occurred between last night up until now simmer in. How could I let this happen? I thought as I but my hands over my face. Then again, I've been so good to Rell and all he does is play with my heart. Fuck it — I'm not going to allow myself to feel guilty, especially when I feel like I'm in heaven right now. I'll deal with the consequences later. Let him get a taste of what I've been feeling on plenty of occasions when he was out doing me wrong.* I got up to go to the bathroom, and LaQuan was in the shower. "Would you like a little bit of company?"

"You don't even have to ask that, beautiful."

I joined him in the shower, and he automatically started washing me up all over, especially between my thighs, hitting all the right spots. While he was doing all this to me, I looked at him, wondering, *where have you been all my life?* He looked at me once again as if he knew what I was thinking. I started washing him up just as well, especially that long trunk of his.

He looked at me and said, "So, you think I'm going to let you off that easy?"

"I hope not," I responded, "but let me give you a taste of what I'm working with." I got down on my knees and gave C-Gutta the best professional ever — C-Gutta, that's what I named his dick because it's curved, and it's nasty in a good way. I was going to town on him as the water fell down on us.

"Oh, do the damn thing, baby. You're taking Daddy there beautiful." Once I started humming and stroking on the pipe, that's all she wrote. He began to release uncontrollably. I got up, and we just held each other as the water fell on the both of us. This shit felt like a dream, and I didn't want to wake up. We got out of the shower and got dressed.

"Let's go out for a while," he suggested.

"Okay. Where are we going?"

"Anywhere you want to go. Let's just go."

To my surprise, we ended up at the Gucci Store on Fifth Avenue. "What are we doing here?" I asked.

"I told you, Taraine. I like to live the good life, and I like to buy nice things. Look around and see what you like."

"I can't do that, LaQuan."

"All right, no problem. I'll pick something out for you." He ended up picking up this bad-ass bag with the matching shoes. I started feeling real sick inside; this was crazy—I was definitely not used to this.

"Thank you, baby," I said, giving him a big grateful kiss. We went to eat at the Steak and Lobster House; this was my very first time at this restaurant. We ordered, and talked while we waited for our food to arrive.

"So, Taraine, what's this we got going on?"

"I don't know, LaQuan. I told you I have a man, although I must be honest with you. What took place between you and I was unbelievable. Usually, you read about this shit in books. You feel me. You know the urban books you read—that's about a regular chick, who hooks up with a hustler, and he goes out and spends lots of money on her, takes her on expensive trips, and buys her the nice rides, etc., etc. I'm not calling you a drug dealer or anything like that, but that's how I feel right now. You understand what I'm saying."

"Yeah, I do," he said. "I can't explain it, Taraine. It's as if we were supposed to meet, and I'm trying not to let you slip away."

"Are you willing to deal with the fact that I have a man at home?" I asked him.

"I'm not a home-wrecker, but I'm willing to show you that I'm the man you need in your life."

"Damn, you make me not want to go home. You got me feeling as if I should just take my baby and run." I started feeling a little bad because Rell had just started showing me that he was willing to do whatever it took to keep our family together. But then again, just a couple of months ago he was doing me wrong. I explained to LaQuan all I'd been through with Rell and that I was really fed up.

"You know what, beautiful? We could just take our time and see how things work out. You definitely seem like someone I would like to get to know better. As I told you before, Taraine, I'm single. I don't come with any extra baggage. I'm into pleasing my woman I enjoy making her feel special I love treating my woman like a queen. I'm not perfect, but I am a hell of a catch, and I hope you stick around to see all I have to offer. I always meet women who don't appreciate being treasured the way a woman should be. They love drama and negative attention. That's not me; I'm not violent toward woman, and I'm never disrespectful."

"Maybe because you did to them what you just did to me. You fucked me good and then you bought me expensive gifts without getting to know who I was first. Don't get me wrong, because I love everything that happened between us in such a little bit of time, and it feels like I've known you for a very long time. I know where you're coming from, because I'm the same way. I do shit from the heart because that's just who I am. Like you said, there's a reason we connected. It was meant for you to do my party. I gave my heart to Rell, every bit of it, but he put me through hell. The type of relationship Rell and I have, I longer want. I am too much of a classy woman to be going through bullshit every other day.

"To be honest with you, I did give the goods up fast to Rell, but when I dealt with Rell, it was all about him, I never disrespected our relationship by stepping out on him. Plenty of times, I wanted to leave him, but I was so afraid of the unknown—the 'what if's' stay in the back of my mind all the time. What if I found another man just as ignorant as he was? What if he used and abused me like Rell did? Meeting you at the party and the way you were seducing me on the floor had me feeling like we were already together. Damn, LaQuan, you were definitely doing your thing baby, whoa, it still send chills through my body. Anyway, do you have any kids?"

"None that I'm aware of, but there could be a little LaQuan out there." He said.

"Could be, huh?" I said. "Well, just don't let me find out there is a baby, and he's two years old."

He looked at me in confusion?

"We'll talk about that later."

"So we got something special going on, right, Beautiful?"

"I guess we do, Black Stallion."

"Good, because I wasn't trying to let you go just like that anyway. I'm going to show you what real love is supposed to feel like."

"Are you?" I said, blushing.

"You'll see."

We went back to his house, played some music, and relaxed. I was so much in the moment, and I wasn't ready to leave, but I knew I had to go home eventually. Nicera was all right; I knew my mother was taking good care of her.

"What's wrong, baby?" he asked.

I guess I had a concerned look on my face. "I'm a little worried about what's going to go down when I finally go home."

"You'll be all right, beautiful."

"It's not that simple, LaQuan. I'm acting out of character right now so I know Rell knows I'm up to no good by now.

When he did shit to me, I could feel it all in my stomach. That saying, 'follow your gut feeling,' is oh, so true."

"You want me to take you home?"

"No!"

"I don't want to make matters worse, and I definitely don't want anything to happen to you."

"Let's not talk about it. I don't want to spoil what we got going on right now. Whatever is going to happen will happen." I laid my head on his legs and watched TV. I felt so comfortable; I felt like this was how it was supposed to be. I'm not trying to let him go, just to allow some other ungrateful bitch get a hold of him. For the first time, I was going with my gut feeling, and it was telling me he's a keeper.

I ended up falling asleep. He woke me up and said, "Let's go to bed." He grabbed me by my hand and led me to his bedroom. He laid me in the bed and placed the covers over me; he kissed me on my lips and said, "Not to worry about a thing. You got a real man in your life now."

I was awakened by a nice, strong, stiff pipe thrusting my insides with so much passion. Every stroke reminded me of why I had to end my relationship with Rell. I guess LaQuan wanted to send me home nice and satisfied. He wanted to remind me what I had waiting on me. He definitely showed me an unforgettable weekend. Now I had to prepare myself for battle.

Chapter 7

I Did It—So What?

He dropped me off near Fatima's house, where I'd left my car parked. "So when am I going to see you again, beautiful?"

"Well, unfortunately, I have to go to work tonight."

"I'll call you."

"Don't be out there seducing any bitches at them parties."

He started laughing. "You crazy girl."

"No, I'm not crazy. I'm dead-ass serious. Don't get a bitch fucked up."

"I got you, baby. Trust me; I'm not on it like that. I know the way we met was a little crazy, but like I explained to you before, we have a connection. I'm feeling you, and I want to give us a try. I'm going to make you forget about the man who unfortunately is, your baby father."

I started laughing and asked, "Are you positively sure about that?"

"*Hell, yeah!* You're a bad bitch, Taraine, and I'm going to make you mine."

I gave him a little tongue. "You're right—this is just the beginning." I got in my car and drove off to my mother's house.

I walked into my mother's apartment, and Nicera was in her walker. She came running toward me like a little speed demon.

"What's up, Deb?"

"Girl, what are you doing?" she said.

"Why, what happened?"

"You know that knucklehead man called here this morning."

"What did you tell him?"

"Nothing; I didn't answer."

"Good," I said. All I could think about was LaQuan and how he'd turned me out this weekend; he definitely rocked my world.

Rell was only getting a taste of his own medicine. I didn't do this on purpose—shit just happened, and I didn't regret a thing. I wasn't going to worry about it, but in the back of my mind, I knew it was going to go down. It was going to be on and popping when I got home.

He should be at work now, so this is the perfect time to go home. My gut feeling was telling me to leave Nicera with Deb, but I knew my mother needed a little break before I went to work.

I walked in my house, and everything was calm and quiet. *Good; he went to work,* I thought.

Wrong. That motherfucker came out of the bedroom, yelling and screaming like he'd lost his damn mind. "Where the fuck was you at?"

"Rell, why are you all up in my face, first of all?"

"I asked you a fucking question."

"You know where I was, Rell. Tima threw me a party. I stayed with her, and then I went to my mother's house."

"You think I'm fucking stupid, Taraine. Do I look stupid to you?"

"Rell, I don't know what the fuck you're bitching about."

"Two fucking days, your ass been gone. Two days, your ass been out there ho-hopping. Every time you get around your cousins, you lose your mind."

"I ain't lose a damn thing. I was doing me for a change. Rell we need a break to be honest, you're out of control. The roles are reversed for once, and you can't handle it. When you were leaving the house early in the morning and coming back whenever you felt like it, that wasn't a problem. You didn't care about my feelings. Why is it that you can do whatever the hell you want, sleep with whoever the fuck you want, whenever you want and it's okay? But as soon as you think another man is sticking his dick in me, you're all paranoid. Understand this, Rell—you walk around here like your God's gift to me, like you're the only man on earth. You're not the only man who finds me attractive, who wants to treat me good, or—for that matter—who wants to dick me down. I gave you my all, way before you decided to change your ways. When you were giving me your ass to kiss, I was still trying to be strong and be that faithful woman, even though you didn't deserve it. When you wasn't fucking me, you was fucking Vanessa. So let me ask you this, when you were fucking her, did you give a damn about my feelings? Did you even give me a second thought? Hell No! Hear me and hear me good, Rell. You don't have to stay here; you can leave. So fucking what? I stayed out this weekend and guess what? I had a good time, and if I had to do it all over again, you better believe I would, in a heartbeat. Tima gave me a surprise party with a surprise stripper."

"What did you say, Taraine?"

"You heard what I said. I had a surprise stripper, and he did a wonderful job entertaining ME."

"You probably fucked him."

"Guess what, Rell? You're probably right. Think what you want to think, okay? I'm not going to let you destroy my happiness because you're miserable."

"I'm not miserable, Ma. I'm disappointed that you decided to act like a ho this weekend. You just better be lucky I don't beat your ass."

"No, you better be lucky, but if you got something to bring, Rell, then bring it."

"I'm not going to touch your nasty ass. I'll leave that for the next man."

"If I'm so nasty, Rell, you don't have to stay here. Do us both a favor and get out."

"I'm not going no damn where but let that shit happen again, and see what I do to your ass."

"Ain't a damn thing going to happen to me."

"I'm telling you, Taraine, you better stop playing this fucking game with me!" he yelled as he pointed his finger in my face.

"All I know is that you better get your hands out of my face. Shouldn't you be at work? Because I'm not going through this bullshit with you tonight. You know why, Rell? Because I don't have to. You can think what you like. If you don't like what I did, there's the fucking door. Kick rocks. I pay all the bills up in this bitch." I said as I walked away laughing to myself, *Payback is a bitch, ain't it? Yeah, I was fucking another man this weekend, and I'm going to fuck him again. You might as well consider yourself out of here, bastard.*

<><><>

He never left for work. *Oh, well, I guess he'll be quitting another damn job.* I took Nicera and went into my bedroom to lie down. I was tired as hell. I guess that's what happens when you get worked over all weekend long.

He came to lie down behind me with a stiff dick. *Too fucking bad, because he's not getting NONE of this here.* "You need to get your hand off me." He continued rubbing on my ass, but my mind was on something else: "C-Gutta." I smiled to myself and wondered if I was on LaQuan's mind, the way he was on mine. I needed to check my phone to see if he'd called. Once I realized Nicera had gone to sleep, I dozed off. I woke up to this bastard trying to eat my pussy. He had put Nicera in her crib, and he was trying again to get between my thighs.

"Rell, didn't I ask you to stop? I'm tired, and I'm definitely not letting you taste this, especially after the way you talked to me today." I know rejecting him really made me suspect, but so what? Let him go sleep with the drama queen his baby mama. I was just dicked down like never before, and I was trying to hold on to this feeling for as long as I could.

Once he didn't get a response from me, he gave up.

"Taraine, I don't know what I did to you, baby, but you got to give me a little credit, because I'm trying, baby. Baby, please don't do me this way. You're hurting me. I really love you girl."

I could feel his pain in a way, but I didn't want him touching me. "I'm sorry, Rell," I said nonchalantly. "You know I have to go to work, so please let me get some sleep." He finally left me alone. The time flew by so fast, and it was time for me to get ready for work. I got Nicera dressed and took her back to my mother's house. I knew by the time I got in from work, he'd be sleeping, with only an hour left before he had to go to work. I would sleep on the couch until then. I'd do whatever it took to keep him off me. LaQuan was a good—no, great—fuck, but I really didn't know what our future held.

How fucked up can I be? What's wrong with me? Was I wrong for wanting to be with LaQuan? It was all so confusing but I knew this was love at first sight and I had to give it a try.

When I got to work, I went to speak to my supervisor to request a shift change. School was over for the summer, and the night shift wasn't agreeing with me. Work was good, but I was always tired as hell.

When I exited my place of employment, the first thing I saw was that cream BMW. I started smiling as I walked to his car. "What are you doing here, baby?"

"I just got off so I wanted to surprise you." I got in the car I hugged him, like I hadn't seen him in years.

"I wanted to make sure you were all right. I called your phone a couple of times, but it went straight to voicemail."

"I'm alright. We got into it. He tried to get up in my jewel but I rejected his ass and of course, he was tight."

"Baby, I will understand if you don't want to do this. It will hurt me because I'm feeling you, but I don't want any trouble to come your way."

"It's a little too late for that, LaQuan, and I'm feeling you just the same." I reached over hugged him and whispered in his ear, "I'm not trying to let you go baby.

So how was work?" I asked.

"It was all right."

"Just all right? Were you thinking about me?"

"You've been on my mind ever since we departed."

"I'm going to pay you a surprise visit at your job one night also. I want to see how you work the stage. I want to see just how crazy these bitches get for your fine ass."

"That's cool, but don't get mad at what you see."

"Oh, trust me, I will get mad, and I will beat a bitch ass if I have to. Are you taking me home with you?" I asked.

"Of course you're going home with me."

I thought, *Here we go again,* but I couldn't pass this up; I enjoyed being with his fine ass. "You know what's going to happen if I go home with you, right?"

"Nothing," he said. "We're going to get some good sleep. I know I'm tired. What about you?"

I looked at him like, *Yeah, right.* "Stop playing, Boo-Bear."

"Boo-Bear?" he said. "Where did that come from?"

"When I look at you, you're so manly but adorable, and your body—oh … my … God!"

"That's cool," he said, "but when I'm hitting the right spot, you'll be calling me Daddy. Just like you were doing all weekend."

"Oh, you think so."

"I know so," he said.

"Let me get my car, and I'll follow you to your place."

We got back to his place and immediately started going at it.

"Wait, Boo, before we go too far, I need to refresh all this right here."

He looked at me and started laughing. "You're the real deal, girl. Go handle your business." He kissed me on the nose and walked down the hall. "I'll make a bubble bath for you."

"Stop playing! Would you really do that for me?"

"Of course I would. Like I told you before, I'm going to show you how a woman should be treated."

"LaQuan, I'm already into you. You can stop being extra now."

"I'm not being extra, beautiful. This is me, and I'm not trying to change who I am. Don't get scared now."

"I'm sorry. I'm just not used to this, but I do believe I know something good when it's right before my eyes. Trust me—I'm going to keep my guard up because this feels too good to be true, but I'm going to accept what God has put before me. I hope I make you feel just as good and just as special."

He kissed me and said, "Of course you do. You make me feel even better."

I got into my bubble bath that he fixed for me. Oh, it felt so good to relax and soak and not worry about hearing no bullshit in the next room. He came into the bathroom and started washing me up. This man really had me falling in love with him—it was scary. "LaQuan, I don't know if I told you this before but no man has ever made me feel the way you have in such a short period of time."

"Is that a good thing or a bad thing?" he asked.

"It's a great thing, and I definitely appreciate the experience and the love. It's so good to know there's still good men out here. Baby, I am so tired. This night shift can be draining at times."

"Stand up, beautiful, so I can dry you off and put you to bed."

I must have really been tired, because I didn't wake up until around noon. I turned and looked over at LaQuan sleeping, and I thought, *I would really love to have a future with this man. In just a short period of time, he has changed me, changed my way of thinking. How could this be?*

I didn't understand this at all; it still felt like a dream. I didn't care how Rell felt. I was waiting for him to leave and go back to his baby mother for good.

I decided to get up and make him something to eat show him I had some skills in the kitchen as well. I opened the refrigerator, it was surprisingly full. *Damn, what's up with this man? Is he married? Is he gay? Is he ...* I couldn't think of anything else. *Fuck it, enjoy it while it's good, girl.* "Wake up, baby," I said, shaking him gently.

"What's this?" he said.

"Get up and eat." I cooked him some steak and shrimp I found in your fridge, with potatoes, broccoli, and cheese.

"Damn, baby, you just threw down in my kitchen, restaurant-style, huh."

"Yes, I did. You better enjoy this because I don't do this for just anybody. I tried to show you that, the morning you cooked breakfast for me, but I was kindly interrupted by C-Gutta."

"Interrupted, huh?"

"Yes, but a good interruption," I said as I winked at him. "I want you to meet my family."

"When?"

"Today, if you have the time."

"Are you sure?" he asked.

"I'm positive; trust me." I called my mother to let her know I was on my way.

"Deb, I'm on my way to pick up Nicera, and I'm bringing a friend."

"Did you call Rell?"

"No, why?"

She didn't answer.

"Debra, I'm enjoying my life, and I'm not letting Rell hold me back any longer."

"I'm just telling you to be careful."

"I know, Deb. I'll be there soon."

We got to my mother's house, and I introduced them. "LaQuan, this is my mother, Debra, and Debra, this is the new man in my life, LaQuan." Then I took him over to Nicera. "This is my little princess I've been telling you about." I turned to my mother. "So what you think about this chocolate hunk right here?"

She just smiled. He and my mother talked while I got Nicera dressed. "Are you bringing her back here tonight, or are you leaving her with Rell?"

"You know I am not leaving my child with his ass, but I'm not going in tonight anyway. I'll call you later on, and if Rell calls, just ignore him."

"We're going back home with you LaQuan, if that's all right with you."

"Of course it's all right with me." LaQuan said smiling.

Even though my feelings were dying fast for Rell, I still had love for him. I was just tired of going through all the drama. I knew I'd asked him to change, but "shit happens" for a reason and maybe his change came too late.

Chapter 8

I Moved On

Nine months passed, and LaQuan and I were tighter than ever. We did everything together. We went on cruises—he took me to Cancun and Atlantis in the Bahamas; we were just doing it up big. Eventually, Rell found out about LaQuan. He was still suspicious about how I was moving, but he could never pinpoint anything until Fatima opened her big-ass mouth, probably on purpose. To be honest she really did me a favor by telling Rell. Did Rell leave when she told him? Hell, no, he didn't leave. Oh, well, I really didn't care what Rell knew. I was not leaving LaQuan. Rell hadn't taste this pussy ever since he tried that weekend I was with LaQuan. I rejected him then, and I would reject him if he tried it now, I just wanted him to leave my house.

In these last couple of months, my man had done more for me than Rell had done in all of our years together—not just financially but in every way, mentally and physically. He is the type of man you would love to take home to Mama, and Debra loved her some LaQuan.

It was to the point where I was never staying home. I was always at LaQuan's house. I decided to go home to get us some clothes. As soon as I walked in the door, his ass was ready to argue. I was used to the arguing, but this time was different. All I saw was a fist coming to my jaw and then a kick to my stomach.

"I hate you, bitch. Why are you cheating on me?"

"Oh, motherfucker, I know you didn't just punch me in my face."

"Yeah, I did, ho."

I pushed Nicera into the living room, went straight to the counter drawer, and pulled out a knife. "You dumb motherfucker; didn't I tell you to never put your hands on me again?"

"I'm tired of you, Taraine. I'm so fucking tired of your shit." Damn I knew payback was a bitch because he sounded the same way I used to sound when I got at him for cheating on me or doing me wrong; all those times when I was begging for him to treat me and Nicera right. He didn't care about how much he hurt me or the pain I felt.

I managed to get the knife to his throat. "Rell, if you ever put your hands on me again, I swear to God I will slice your fucking throat. I don't want to go to jail, but trust me, I will if I have to." The only thing that took me out of this trance was Nicera's crying. I needed to get my baby and get the hell out of this house.

"You call yourself a good mother, and you got my daughter up in some other nigga's face."

"Rell, how much attention do you give to Nicera?" I shouted as the tears rolled down my face.

"You're a fucking nasty bitch, Taraine. Where's your man at now?"

"None of your damn business." I said

"As a matter of fact, you got one minute to get the fuck out before I call the police."

"I told you before—I'm not going no fucking where. You want me out? Tell your man to come kick me out. Call the cops, you dirty bitch, and while you're at it, tell them you're a fucking ho. I should spit in your fucking face."

"You spit in my face, Rell, and it will be the last face you ever spit in."

"You ain't worth it, bitch," he said.

"I must be worth it you're still hanging around. I've been begging you to leave for months. I haven't been sleeping with you. We don't talk, and I don't even like you anymore, Rell. You are such a turn off. So, I'll ask you again. Why are you here?"

"Oh, so because you got another dick sliding up in you, I'm a fucking turn off."

"You damn right. He lays it down real good. The first night my man made love to me, he turned me out. Every time he touches me, I catch multiple orgasms. His balls always smell good, unlike yours—sweat and weed. He treats me like a queen. He's my daddy, and trust me, my pussy is well adjusted to his curved dick. Yes, he's packing, and when we're getting it on, I scream all kind of things to let him know, he got it going on. I can go on and on, but it's self-explanatory. I'm not trying to pull the wool over your eyes, Rell. I love him; as a matter of fact, I'm in love with him, and there's not a damn thing you can do to change that."

"Taraine, shit always seems good in the beginning."

"Maybe so, Rell, but I will never have to worry about him putting his hands on me, stealing from me, and I definitely won't have to worry about him cheating on me."

"How do you know he's not cheating on you?"

"Well, if he is, it's hard to tell, and he's doing a good job at it. He gives me the utmost respect. That's all I ever wanted from you, Rell, was respect and to be treated like a lady. I bent over backwards for you, and that's all I ever wanted in return."

"I did change, Ma."

"How? By punching me in my face as soon as I walk in the door? That shit ain't cool. Please believe that if I call him over here, he will come to tear your ass up, but Rell, I know how you rock. I know you're a punk, so I'm not going to waste his time with your bullshit."

"Well, why don't you go live with him?"

"Rell, this is my apartment, and if anybody is leaving, it's going to be you."

"You know I ain't got no place to go, Taraine."

"Go to your mother's house, or go to the drama queen's house. I really don't give a fuck where you go, just get the fuck out."

"Ma, I never thought the day would come when I see you on another man's dick."

"Oh, really? Well, trust me; I'm on it, and I'm on it hard. I suck it well, and I ride it well." Before I knew it, he had slapped me again, and I came back with it, cutting him right across his arm. I was about to lose my mind. *No, girl, don't let him take you there.* I grabbed Nicera and walked towards my door. "I want you out of my apartment, Rell. I don't love you anymore, and I don't know if I ever really loved you. *It's over!*"

Chapter 9

Da Disappearance

After about a week or so, Rell finally moved out. I guess he realized it was really over. I changed the locks once he was gone. I continued to stay with LaQuan for a while because I didn't trust Rell at all.

Around the holidays, LaQuan was working extra hard and doing more parties. That was definitely one thing I could say about him—he was about his business in a positive way. He liked making money and having lots of cars. He was focused on getting rich; he was a hustler but in a legit way. LaQuan's cousin Lance had moved up to NYC from Philly and was staying with LaQuan until he got on his feet. They could pass for twins, but of course, my baby looked much better. They began doing private parties together, too. He was all right; he seemed to be about his business like LaQuan, but there was something about him I didn't trust.

It was almost our one-year anniversary. LaQuan was planning something special for us. He just told me to make sure my mother was able to keep Nicera for at least a week or two for us.

Rell had finally fallen back; he wasn't stressing me out anymore. I guess he finally got the point. He was telling anyone who would listen how this bitch-ass nigga took his family from him and how he was going to get us back.

I don't think he really wanted me back. I just think he wanted to be the one to do the hurting. I guess I just beat him to it, so his ego was crushed.

Lance's moving in put a little damper on me and LaQuan's sex-capades, at least at his house. We had to be cautious about where, when and how we put it down. I know he heard us all the time, because at times we got pretty frisky forgetting he was in the house. We didn't hold anything back when it came to sex. I loved backstrokes, and he loved how it made my ass clap. He loved the way my ass moved, it was doing its own dance with every stroke.

"Oh, Moc, look at how that ass is bouncing for Daddy."

Oh, yeah, that was my new nickname. I loved when he called me "beautiful," but you can call anybody beautiful. That's right; give me my own shit. He just looked up at me and said, "I love your skin, Mocha Chocolate. You got to give me another name, because that Boo-Bear shit is too fruity.

I'm not changing your name 'cause that's what you are." Deep down inside, I think he liked it, but when I called him Daddy, he liked it even more, especially when he was doing the damn thang.

The more I got to know Lance, the more suspicious he appeared to be. I couldn't put my finger on it, but I wasn't really feeling him anymore. I didn't tell LaQuan, because I didn't want to start no bullshit, but he could tell something was up by my actions around him. Plus, I started spending fewer nights at his house.

"LaQuan, when is Lance going to find his own place? Or is he becoming your permanent roommate?"

"Nah, he is going back to Philly. Why? What happened?"

"Nothing. I'm just being nosey, and I must admit I was missing our kitchen, living room, hallway, and bathroom sessions. I love when you start getting real aggressive on me. I love when you pull my hair, and tell me to shut up and take the dick.

Oooh-wee, Daddy that shit turns me on." I looked at him and started smiling. "You are so nasty, Daddy."

"You're the one that said it, so why am I the nasty one?"

"Well, he has to hurry up and get the fuck out."

"Come here, Moc. Don't worry; he'll be out of our way sooner than you think."

<><><>

LaQuan was right. Lance was leaving for Philly next week; he told me he missed his girl. He was going to buy her a diamond tennis bracelet and an engagement ring before he went back home. We were going away next week, too, so I knew LaQuan was glad. I doubt he wanted to leave Lance in his house for a whole week or more.

The week went by fast. I found myself home, packing my bags. I had dropped Nicera off to my mother's house.

The phone rang. "What's up, Moc? You ready?"

"Almost"

"All right, I'm going to pick you up in about two hours. I'm going to take Lance to the diamond district, and then he's leaving for Philly."

"All right, that's cool. I'll definitely be ready by then."

"I love you, Moc."

"I love you, too, Daddy."

Two hours passed, and no LaQuan. *Okay, he's late. That's unusual for him.* He would at least call. I called his phone but got his

voicemail. My stomach started to twist on the inside—
something was wrong. *Don't panic, bitch. We won't miss our flight.*

Another hour passed—and still no LaQuan. I called his
phone and still no answer. "LaQuan, baby, I'm waiting on you.
What's the deal, Daddy? Call me back."

Now I was pacing back and forth. *Where the fuck is he?* I sat
down. I got back up. I must have called his phone a thousand
times, and I wasn't reaching him. Another hour passed, and
we'd missed our flight.

I called my mother. "Deb, did LaQuan call there?"

"No, I thought y'all were on the plane by now."

"No, I'm still waiting. He never called me back. Something's
not right Deb." After I hung up with my mother, I started
calling the hospitals and precincts. "Do you have a LaQuan
Cummings there?" One by one, they all said no.

Now I was really going into panic mode. I hope Rell didn't
try anything stupid, I thought. Nah, Rell ain't got the heart, but
you can't put anything past a scared man. *I'm nervous as hell
right now.*

His phone was still ringing, and then going right to
voicemail. I decided to call Lance's phone—the same shit; ring
and then voicemail. I called the hospitals, looking for Lance, but
I couldn't remember his last name to save my life. *Damn! What
is his last name?* I cried and cried until my eyes began to swell.

I decided to go to his house. When I got there, I didn't see
his Yukon, but I did see his BMW. I walked into his apartment.
Nothing looked strange or out of place. His bags were gone, but
he had two outfits on the bed, which looked like he'd decided
not to bring them on the trip. I stood there, puzzled, like, where
is he? I looked in the closet where he kept his safe. I opened it
up, and it still had all his money inside. He has been saving his
money so he could start his own construction company. *"What
the fuck?"* I screamed at the top of my lungs.

I left his apartment and went to After Dark, the club where
he worked.

Nobody had seen him since the night before. I decided to go to the hospitals and precincts to show them his picture. "Still nothing" I went back to my house and cried. *What kind of games are you playing, LaQuan?* Everything went through my mind in a flash, until finally ... "No, no, no I screamed, as I dialed the last number no one would ever want to dial—the morgue. Just dialing the number gave me the chills."

Hello.

"Yes, I'm calling to find out if by chance you have a twenty-eight-year-old African American male there by the name of LaQuan Cummings." While I was waiting for her to respond, it felt like my heart had dropped to my feet.

"Let me check, Miss. please hold." It seemed like it took her an eternity to get back to the phone. "No, I'm sorry—or should I say I'm happy—to say there's no one here by that name."

"Thank you, Miss," I said and hung up the phone. *What the fuck is going on? I know he didn't just drop off the face of the earth. Did he take Lance all the way to Philly? Why is neither of them picking up their damn phone? You know what—let me chill out; he'll be here eventually, even though I'm so scared and upset right now. I have to believe he is all right.*

I cried myself to sleep. I woke up, and it was eight in the morning. I looked at my phone to see if I had any missed calls.

Nope.

I tried to call his cell again, but now it automatically went to his voicemail. I just started bugging out. *Yo, I can't believe this man was doing me dirty all this time, I just can't believe it. Does he have a secret family in Philly he never told me about? When he does come back, I am going to dig in his ass like a sharp knife. I can't let him get away with hurting like this. He thinks he can play this type of game with me and get away with it.*

Oh, hell, no. I know I was talking crazy; I was just hurting and so confused. I didn't know what was going on. "Why, baby, why?" I just cried and cried with my face buried in my pillow. I called my mother. "Hey, Deb, we never made the flight, but can you keep Nicera for a few days?" I explained to her a little bit of what was going on, which was nothing because I didn't know anything my damn self.

His mother and I had a good relationship, but every time I tried to call her, I would get her answering machine. "Hi, Ma, this is Taraine. When you get this message can you give me a call?" I couldn't eat, drink, or sleep. All I wanted to do was see my baby, my man, my daddy.

Come home, baby, please come home. Please be all right so I can kill you after for putting me through this heartache and pain.

I started questioning God. *Why did you give me someone special, besides Nicera, and then take him away? Is this my punishment for hurting Rell? God, I didn't hurt him on purpose. I just felt you sent me my king, and I needed to get rid of the low life that was bringing me down. Please, God, just let him be all right. I'm begging you.*

Then the phone rang. I raced quickly to answer it.

"Hello, LaQuan?"

"No, this ain't no bitch-ass LaQuan."

"Not now, Rell," I said and hung up.

He called back, but I let it go straight to voicemail. He continued calling, back to back, until finally I picked up.

"Why are you calling my house like a crazed maniac?"

"I just called to see—"

I got mad and cut him off. "Called to see what, Rell?"

He laughed hysterically. "What's wrong with you? Your man did you wrong already."

"What?"

"You heard me, Ma."

"What do you want, Rell?"

"Nothing. Forget it, Ma."

"Get a life Rell." I yelled and hung up.

I got back in my bed. *Why is Rell calling me all of a sudden? We haven't been in contact for months. I know he better not have anything to do with LaQuan's disappearance.*

I showered, got dressed, and went back to LaQuan's house. Everything was still the same. I could tell no one had been there. I looked in the closet, and it was still untouched. *Take the safe out the closet, girl,* I thought. I called Tima. "Girl, I need a favor."

"What, chica?"

"I need you to help me get this safe out of LaQuan's closet and take it to my house. I'll talk to you when you get here." This safe was not going to fit into my car, so I decided to use Fatima's truck. When she got to the house, I explained everything to her. She was just as shocked as I was. She called a mutual friend to see if he had heard anything. She worked for City Corrections, so I told her maybe she could get one of her co-workers to check and see if he was in the system.

She made a couple of calls but came up with nothing.

"Tima, I called everywhere I could think of and came up blank. I don't know what to do. My baby is MIA, but the weirdest thing about it is he left all his money behind. Even if he was leaving me, he wouldn't leave his life savings behind. That's how I know something is not right."

"Girl, we can't just walk out with that big ass safe and expect not to get robbed. And further more who told you I wanted to lift that heavy ass safe. What you trying to do get us robbed or killed? Which one"

"All right, let's just take all the money out of the safe. Put it in one of LaQuan's duffle bags." If I was low down and dirty, I would just say fuck it, and Tima and I would spend this damn money, but that's not me. I would trade all this money in just to have him here, right in front of me, knowing he was all right. "You know that bastard Rell called me this morning, too, and I haven't spoken to him since I changed the locks on the door. I don't know if it's just a coincidence or not."

On our way back to my house, I had to tell Tima to pull over. She pulled over, and I opened the door and started throwing up.

"What's wrong with you?"

"I think I got a stomach virus or something."

"No, bitch, I think you're pregnant."

I looked at her, Tima please *stop playing; this ain't no time to be joking around.*

Two weeks passed and still nothing. I had to get back to my life. I still had my daughter to raise and bills to pay. I went to PC Richards and bought another safe; it was smaller but it would do. I was so stressed out. I lost weight and my hair began falling out. I was throwing up every morning since the day Fatima pulled over so that I could puke my guts out. I decided to go to the doctor—and Tima was right; I was pregnant and I had mixed feelings as to what I should do. Everything was still too painful for me. I couldn't understand what the fuck was going on. I knew in my heart that LaQuan wouldn't just do me dirty like this. Things just didn't add up, and I was still on the prowl to get to the bottom of it, no matter what the outcome may be.

LaQuan always paid his rent three months in advance. Every once in a while, I would go over to his apartment to just get a feel of him, to smell him, to have flashbacks of the very first time I went to his house—the very first time we made love. I was miserable. I was missing him like crazy and now I was pregnant with his child. I know people probably thought he was dead, but in my heart, I knew he wasn't.

I decided to keep the baby and move on with my life. His last month of paid rent was almost up, so I decided to start moving his furniture out. By now, I was five months pregnant. The doctor said *it's a boy, but I'm not falling for that, he said the same thing about Nicera, and we went out and bought everything blue.* I rented a moving truck and got a couple of guys to help me move everything to my apartment. I could have just moved into his apartment, but there were too many memories.

When I was in my eighth month of pregnancy, my friends and family gave me a surprise baby shower; it was beautiful. Everybody was there—people I hadn't seen in a while. I know they were dying to ask me questions about LaQuan, but they didn't. I had unanswered questions of my own, so I would be no good to them. Being pregnant this time took away all my beauty. Even though this was supposed to be the happiest time of my life, it wasn't. I pretended a lot of the time—no, all of the time. I went out on maternity leave from my job. While I was out on leave, I had to go into LaQuan's safe and spend some of his money. Well, it was his baby, too. Things happen for a reason; and he had more than enough to share.

I still wasn't eating or drinking right. When I woke up, I felt weak. I called my mother and must have passed out while I was talking to her on the phone, because when I opened my eyes, I realized I was in the hospital with an intravenous in my arm.

"Girl, you got to stop stressing yourself out and get it together so you can bring a healthy baby into this world." Debra said with a concerned look on her face.

I was ready to burst out crying and tell my mother I couldn't do this. All of a sudden, I got this sharp pain in my stomach. I just held my belly and started screaming, the pain was unbearable.

"What's wrong?"

"Oh, it hurts, something is wrong. Go get the doctor please Deb." I screamed.

It seem like they took forever to come back. The doctor checked me and said, "Oh, it looks like this baby is ready to make its grand entrance into the world." I wasn't due yet, but this baby was ready to come, and the contractions were letting me know this was the real deal.

This baby was more difficult than Nicera. It seemed like the doctor was yelling push a thousand times. I wanted to say,

"Shut up, and get this damn baby out of me! Listen, you little stubborn child, why are you putting me through so much pain." I yelled

I pushed and pushed until finally I could hear my baby crying. I looked over at Deb, and she smiled with joy.

"What is it?"

"It's a girl."

"It is?" I said, crying. "Let me see my baby." I watched them clean her up, and then they handed her to me. "Look at you; look at my baby," I said as I kissed her on her cheek and then her hand. She had a head full of curly hair. "Hey, Raine," I said, kissing her on her little hands. She was the cutest thing ever. LaQuan said if he ever had a girl, her name was going to be Raine Lanae Cummings, and so it was. She was so adorable. I fell in love with my baby, but I was tired as hell. I tried to give her breast milk but she refused to accept it.

Later on that day, I was surprised to see LaQuan's mother walk into my hospital room. She had lost a lot of weight, and she was looking just as stressed out as I was.

I said, "Ma, this is your granddaughter, Raine."

"She looks just like her father."

Hearing her say that made me sad all over again. "Have you heard anything, Ma?"

"No," she said real fast, but her "no" was kind of a suspicious no, as if she was hiding something.

"Anyway, I can't put all my thoughts into it right now. I got a new bundle of joy to raise—his bundle of joy."

<><><>

Two days later they let us go home. Everything was set up real nice. The baby had come a little early, but I was glad to welcome her into this world. I just held her in my arms and cried until I couldn't cry anymore. When I got myself together, I looked over at Nicera, who was looking at me as if she could tell

I was hurting. "Come here, Nicera." She walked slowly to me. I picked her up and kissed her. "I love you, Cee-Cee. Did you miss Mommy?" She shook her head yes and giggled. My phone rang.

"Hello."

"What's up, Ma?"

"What's up, Rell. I'm not in the mood for no arguing today."

"Nah, I just called to say congratulations on your new baby—the baby that should have been mines."

"Thank you," I said.

"How's my daughter?"

"She's fine. When are you going to start taking care of her? I'm giving you a chance to do it on your own before I take your ass to court."

"You can take me wherever you want to take me. You're just another statistic, like all the rest of them hoes. You're a simple-ass ho with two kids and no baby father around."

I couldn't even argue with his ass. My response to him was, "Thank you. I'll see you in court. Tell it to the judge."

Chapter 10

Get Through Da Pain

Time seemed to go by so fast. Raine was almost nine months old. My life had changed drastically, and I needed to find a way to get out of this slump I was in.

I decided to take a test for something I never thought I would do, which was Corrections. That was Fatima's thing, not mines, but the jobs out here weren't paying enough for me to support my family. I was getting ready to graduate from college with my BA in Psychology. How I managed to get through college in the past year surprised me, but I thanked God for my family's help and support.

For some reason, Fatima stopped having our venting sessions, and we needed to have one immediately. I needed a little bit of help, trying to get back on track. I could have tried getting with another man, but the only man I wanted was LaQuan.

I decided to put the session together myself. Everybody showed up—Fatima, Kelly, Shantae, and Slim. I cooked everything, and I bought the drinks so we were straight for the night.

"So, what's up, ladies? I called for this session because I desperately need to vent. It's a lot of shit that I've been going through, and I've been holding it in for far too long," I said as I burst out crying. "I miss my baby. I don't know where, how, when, or why, but my baby is gone, and it's killing me."

"We can tell girl," Kelly said. "You don't even look like yourself. When we talk on the phone, it's like you're not even there, mentally."

"Y'all just don't understand. My man and his fucking cousin just vanished. My stomach doesn't sit right with that. He left his safe full of money. What person is just going to break out and leave all their money in a safe? Every time I look at Raine, she reminds me of LaQuan more and more. She is the splitting image of him. I need to get back into doing things to keep myself focused and occupied. We need to throw some parties and trips."

They all agreed.

"I don't want to make this all about me, but I need serious help, because I feel like I'm going to have a nervous breakdown. I am really depressed, guys. I know my baby is not dead; I can feel him, there's a spiritual connection we have. My baby is alive and nobody can tell me anything different." I said as the tears flowed

What's going on with y'all?"

"Where do I start?" Slim said. "Sometimes I wonder why I married my husband. I wonder if it was all for love, or did I just want all that money he was offering me to help him get his green card? Now that he has his green card, he always tries to make me feel like I'm worthless. He's always ranting Yankee this and Yankee that." She mimicked him in a West Indian accent. "I wanted to say, 'If it wasn't for this Yankee right here, you wouldn't even be here, unless you found some other bimbo to marry your ass.' One morning I was going through his phone and found a picture of a naked woman. I confronted him. Of course, he got upset and started hitting me like I was his personal punching bag. I packed up some clothes for me and the kids, and I left him."

"What?" we all said in shock.

"He had the nerve to keep proof of the foul shit he was doing?" Fatima asked.

"Hell yeah and then he had the nerve to try and pull reverse psychology on me. Now he's calling my mother's house constantly."

"That's why I don't fuck with men anymore," Shantae said, tight as hell.

"No more dick." I said.

"*No more dick.*" Shantae said.

"I went to a lesbian/gay bar with one of my co-workers. I didn't go there with the intentions of meeting a chick, but one of them caught my eye, and we've been kicking it for a minute now, and this bitch is *bad*."

"So, what's it like?" nosey-ass Fatima said.

"Yeah, what's it like to be with a woman?" Slim asked.

"Wait—who's the woman? You or her" Fatima asked

"Well, we're both diva lesbians, but I'm a little more aggressive than she is. I will put on the strap and fuck her with no problem."

Fatima was like, "Oh no, no, no, bitch! I couldn't do that; I'm strictly dickly." Fatima had this arrogance about her that sometimes would make you want to knock her ass out.

That was the way of the world now; it didn't matter if you agreed with it or not. This was reality and either you agreed or disagreed with the lifestyle. I really didn't care as long as no one tried coming at me.

Kelly started laughing. "So what made you decide to be with a woman?"

"Just talking to this chick turned me on. I used to talk to a lot of lesbians over the internet but I never pursued it until I met the girl at the bar. I was infatuated with her; just talking to her was different. It felt different but it felt right, we connected."

"You go down on her and all that?" I asked.

"Yeah, it's not the greatest taste in the world, but I get the job done. She's always satisfied."

"Look at this shit," Slim said sarcastically. "You eating bitches out but I can't even get my husband to blow on mines."

"What do you mean; it's not the greatest thing in the world?" Kelly said.

"Please try to understand me on a different level," Shantae said. "When I'm in the mood, I don't think about the taste, or other things that happens with us down there because I'm horny and I'm getting off from just pleasing her alone, but there have been times when I would just rather find another way to please her."

"What's the difference between tasting a man and tasting a woman?" Fatima said.

"A man is an outer, and a when he's ready to cum, usually he'll react, and if a woman gets a little bit of it in her mouth, she's running fast to spit that shit out, unless she gets down like that."

"Not me," Kelly said. "I take that shit to the motherfucking head. I ain't running, spitting shit out."

"Bitch, you so nasty, but I can't front—I tried it once with LaQuan, when I was really in a freaky mood. I feel like this: you have to be fun and spontaneous with your man, 'cause trust me—what you don't do, the next bitch will. That's another reason why I know something went wrong with LaQuan, because we was getting it in; our sex game was great. We were trying all type of shit. Videotaping, using toys—you name it, we did it. Our sex life was exciting. He tried positions on me I never knew existed. We all experience different things and I know everything's not for everybody. Everything I tried, I was comfortable doing and I never regretted it."

"Don't knock it until you try it," Kelly said, giving me dap as the rest of the girls looked at her.

"Why the fuck y'all looking at me like that? Y'all bitches know I'm nasty, and I don't give a damn, but besides being a freak, I got issues, y'all. I'm tired of Keith. At times I love him, and then there are times when I just want to say fuck everything. We have been together so long and done so much bullshit together. I'm afraid he'll try to end my career if I leave him, which leaves me stuck between a rock and a hard place. We use to have that unbreakable connection, but now he treats me like it's his way or no way at all.

"I've tried everything with him—had threesomes, went to strip clubs—you name it, we tried it. We fucked any and everywhere—even got caught by the police a couple of times. We got sex toys galore, but that's all he wants to do is have sex 24/7, and argue, then have sex some more. He wants to be in control of everything. He refuses to let me be my own woman; he refuses to let me do me. Every time we argue, he wants to involve the kids.

"The last time I called the cops, they refused to take him out of the house. It's ridiculous, and I'm tired of it. By the cops refusing to take him out of the house—that makes him feel like he has more control over me. I can do it all without him, but he tries to make me feel like I can't make it without him. Y'all just don't understand how bad I want out of this relationship. It's driving me crazy.

"When that situation happened in Albany, they locked me up because I was trying to hold my man down, which left me six months pregnant and locked up. You would think he would be showing me all the love in the world just for doing time for something he had done. I told him I went to jail for him, and I held it down, pregnant and all, but I'm wondering if he would have done the same for me. Probably not, because lately, I've been seeing a lot of bitch in him, which was probably already there, but my dumb ass was blind to the fact that my man could be a bitch."

"See, that is why I do me," Fatima said. "My one true love Al loved the street life too much, and now he's not here anymore. I don't give a fuck about all these other motherfuckers. I fuck them and leave them. He can take me out, take me shopping, buy me all type of nice shit, but I'm not falling for him. Why? To have him break my heart in the long run?"

"What about family?" Kelly said.

"No disrespect, but fuck family. You, Taraine, and Slim— y'all live that family life shit, and there's still turmoil. I would rather have the turmoil with just me. I wouldn't want to put any kids through the motion, so fuck family values."

"What about falling in love, Tima?" I asked.

"Taraine, don't play with me. You know I was in love, and now he's gone. He left me with a broken heart."

Her man finally came home and was killed by some people he thought he was cool with; he went way back with, as he would say, his boys for life. "They say time heals everything, right?" I said.

"Ask yourself that, Taraine."

"I guess you're right, Tima. I got the chance to know what real love felt like when I started dealing with LaQuan. His love was pure, and it was definitely from the heart."

"And guess what, chica? He's gone, and you're stuck here with a broken heart and his child."

To hear her say that left me numb. I excused myself, went into the bathroom, and let it all out. This was the release I needed, but it hurt so bad. I got myself together and went back into the living room with the girls.

"I'm sorry, Taraine. I know my words at times come out too strong, and I'm sorry—I'm so sorry. I just want to say I'm always going to be here for y'all bitches, no matter what."

We held our wine glasses up and toasted to always having each other's backs. There's nothing like a ladies night to help you get through the pain. I love my girls, always and forever.

Chapter 11

Why

I passed the test and was called to be interviewed and investigated for the Department of Corrections. It wasn't my first career choice, but it paid good money. If everything went well, I would start the academy in two or three weeks. My mother agreed to keep the kids for the twelve weeks of training, and I was ready to get it on and popping—at least that's what I thought.

<>< ><>

The first day of training was hell. By the third day, I was calling Deb. "I can't do this; they are driving me crazy up in here. My body is cramping up. I'm not used to working out like this. We woke up four in the morning to run and exercise. Deb, this is not for me."

"You can do it. If the rest of them are all right, you'll be all right also," she said.

"I guess you right. I'll put my best foot forward."

All I kept telling myself was "You can do it!" every time I wanted to give up, which seemed like every day. It was definitely hard being away from the kids. I missed them so much, but I had to do this for them and for their future. Even though I was occupied, I still missed LaQuan and wondered if I would ever see him again. Would God bring him back to me if I prayed hard enough? I knew one thing for sure—he probably wouldn't like my career choice, but he would have held me down to the very end. "Stack money and live good" was his motto, and that's what he was doing—stacking money and living good.

I had only two weeks left before I graduated, and it seemed like forever. The training was getting harder and more intense. I knew one thing for sure: I was definitely in shape. I passed all the written tests and all the obstacles and was ready to graduate.

The graduation ceremony was very nice. I felt so important and very proud of myself for completing the training without giving up. My mother came with Nicera and Raine. Fatima came as well. No matter what, I can always count on her and my mother. After the ceremony, we went out to eat.

I was so glad to be home with my kids. I was so glad to be in my own house, my own bed, and not sharing a room with other trainees. I got the kids ready for bed, and then I took a much-needed hot bubble bath. I got under my comforter with a picture of LaQuan and just stared at it until finally, I fell asleep.

Monday was my first day of working inside a facility. Walking inside of this place and hearing the bars close behind me scared me half to death. I had to tell myself to get a fucking grip and show no fear. I was still in training. I was just doing it from inside the facility and not on the Academy campus. The inmates were looking at all the new officers as if we were worse than shit. They had pure hatred for us without even knowing us.

I just thought, *Bitch, what the fuck did you get yourself into?* The smell alone was enough to drive a person insane—it was a combination of shit, musk, incense oil, and every other thing you could think of, all in one. We were taken on a tour of the facility—the mess hall, the gym, the yard, etc. This place gave me the fucking creeps.

I had my first post, which was working in the mess hall. It was crazy; it felt like the inmates were looking at me with all kinds of shit on their minds. I was probably every kind of bitch, trader, ho, and dyke. The white inmates were probably thinking all of that, too, but most of all, I was just another nigger. The looks they were giving me scared the hell out of me. I felt like I was shrinking right in the spot I was standing in. I had to focus and remember not to let them see me sweat. It's funny—when I was in training, they said to go by the books, but as soon as I graduated and got to the facility, I threw it all out the fucking window, and it became survival of the fittest.

My first day wasn't too bad, but hey, I was only in the mess hall. I didn't get to feel out the rest of the facility as of yet. My shift was finally over, and I was glad to be going home. Just knowing I could walk out the facility eased a lot of tension in my shoulders.

I went to pick up the kids and told my mother about my not-so-bad first day. I explained to her what I had to do in the mess hall, which was basically telling the inmates where to sit, and that they had a certain amount of time they were allowed to eat. I guess that's a way to keep shit moving at a steady pace—not letting the inmates get too comfortable, as if they were dining at Mr. Chow's or some fabulous type of restaurant. In other words, "Eat the damn food, and get the fuck out."

She said, "Well, you made it home in one piece, and that's what counts."

On my way home I bumped into Rell. He didn't spend any quality time with Nicera, but she surely recognized his ass when she saw him.

"Daddy!" she yelled, running to him.

Please, I thought, but I wasn't going to take Nicera's moment of joy away from her. She didn't know her daddy was a dead-beat and a piece of shit.

"What's up, Taraine? I heard you got a new job. You're a fake-ass cop now."

"Call it whatever you want, Rell. I call it stepping up my game for my children. You should try it sometime."

"I'm going to pick her up some things when I get paid," he said. He looked at Raine. "Hey, Lil Ma, I ain't got nothing against you. Your mother did me wrong; you were suppose to be mines."

"Have a nice day, Rell. I have to go."

"Seriously, Taraine, if you need me, just call me."

"All I need is for you to take care of your daughter. Be a fa-ther — that's all I want, nothing else."

"Are you sure about that, Ma?"

"I'm positive," I replied.

"I know you miss me, Ma."

"No, I miss my husband."

He started laughing in an arrogant way. "Who? That bitch-ass nigga who left you pregnant? You thought you had some-thing, didn't you? And what you end up with?"

"You know what I end up with, Rell? Peace of mind. I got love, understanding, and support. I got money in my pocket-book where I left it, and I got treated like a queen."

"Well, you got nothing now," he said.

"Now, that's where you're wrong. I got my beautiful kids, and I got my sanity." I walked off, leaving him standing right there with the dumb look on his face. I went in the house, fed the kids, bathed them, and got them ready for bed. I will admit I did get lonely, but not lonely enough to take that asshole back. *I'll be like Shantae and fuck a woman before I take his grimy, trifling ass back.* Plus, word on the streets was that he was doing the R.

Kelly thing—messing with little girls. Nasty ass—he disgust me. I guess he still didn't have what it took to get a real woman.

It was hard at times, being alone, but I was in no rush to get with anybody. He would have to come much better than LaQuan, and at this moment, I didn't quite see anybody stepping up to the plate like that—at least, not the way he had.

The next day they had me working in the yard. I must admit I wasn't very sociable at this place. It appeared that most of the officers already had their little cliques. Working the yard was all right, but you really had to pay extra attention to everything going on around you. There were too many motherfuckers doing different shit, all at the same time, and anything could jump off at any time. You had some playing basketball, some playing football, some playing cards, some working out or playing handball. The gangs were in their little groups, so your eyes had to be everywhere, all at one time. The thing that bothered me the most was the damn sun. I was roasting out there. I should have been on a beach somewhere with an umbrella over me, relaxing, but my kids and I can't live on the beach, so I had to settle for this fucking yard.

So far everything was going fine. There was a mixture of different attitudes, but the main thing I tried to remember was that I was here to do a job. None of these motherfuckers gave a fuck about you, and don't ever think it's going to be any better because you're a woman. I got to be on my job even more. There were a lot of female corrections officers, but I was new, and they treated me just as that—the new bitch in town.

"Hey, Officer Davis, how you doing today?" one of the inmates said.

"I'm good, thank you." My motto was "You give me respect, and I'll give you the same."

He was a short, Hispanic, older man. There definitely were some who tried to cross the line in the short time that I worked there.

"She's a stuck-up bitch. Fuck her."

Is what I heard but when I turned my head, there was a group of them, so I couldn't tell who had said it. I was still wet behind the ears, so I didn't react. *Don't let them get the best of you. That's all they got is time on their hands.*

When the yard closed, I was sent to do the count. I just prayed I didn't fuck up the count. While I did the count, I turned around and caught some of these fuckers sticking their mirrors through their cell bars — this was how they looked at your ass as you passed their cells.

"Don't let me catch those mirrors, because if I do, they will be mines." I knew they wouldn't stop, but I needed to show some authority and let them know I did have a fucking backbone, female or not. I finished my count and turned it in to the officer in charge of the count board. I was so nervous; I was praying I didn't fuck up. I didn't want to be at fault for a count gone wrong.

"Count clear!" I heard over my radio. Good; I was relieved. For the rest of the day, I really didn't have an assignment; I was an extra. This left me available to any post where I was needed. Jail looked like a dungeon — not saying it's supposed to be a five-star hotel, but damn, this was the worst. I hoped I'd adjust eventually. The only thing about growing up in the projects and then working in a jail is that eventually you'll see somebody you know.

I was posted in the gym. This was much more comfortable than the yard — fewer inmates and less sun. I noticed one inmate just staring at me. He didn't take his eyes off me for one minute. Was this motherfucker crazy? Was he thinking of a way to attack me? So many things went through my mind in a matter of seconds. I got up and checked the gym, or as they say, I made my rounds. Everything seemed cool and on point, so I went back to my quarters. For some reason this guy was still staring me down; then he started walking toward me.

Before he got too close I said, "Is there a problem?"

"You don't recognize me," he said.

"No, I don't. Should I?"

"I know your uncles."

"You don't know my uncles," I said, "because I don't have any uncles." I lied right through my teeth.

"Come on, shorty—you, from Albany projects. I know your uncles Stevie and Jamie."

He was right, but I said, "Sorry, you got the wrong person. You can excuse yourself back into the gym."

Now what should I do? Reporting him is going by the rules, but he really didn't say too much to me. He did know my uncles, but he really didn't know me. *Nah, I'll just play it by ear.* Shit can be so ironic at times. By the end of the day, I recognized a couple of people I went to school with or just knew of.

I continued to work and perform my duties as an officer. I couldn't stand being there. If inmates didn't look at you like you were a piece of meat, they looked at you like they hated the ground you walked on.

Finally, it was my last day at this facility. The next day I had to report to my permanent spot, and I was ready—ready to get the fuck out of this fucking dungeon. The bad part was that I could be going somewhere worse. I'd just pray the next facility was better—at least the smell.

I hoped I would be able to get through the day without breaking down, but I couldn't—it was LaQuan's birthday. I knew he was still alive; I didn't feel death when he came to mind. *Happy Birthday, baby, wherever you are,* I thought. Maybe if I hadn't had a baby by him, getting over him would have been much easier. Probably not, though; he was such a good person. Everything he did was from the heart. *What am I going to tell Raine when she gets older? Your father just fell off the face of the earth?*

"Goddamn you, LaQuan! I'm so fucking mad at you right now!" They say life goes on, but it's kind of hard for me to go on right now. Deep down inside, even though I couldn't see him physically, I could feel him spiritually. This was how I knew we were meant to be; this was why Raine was here. From the very moment he put his move on me at my party—or should I say, fucked me mentally—there was a connection. Sometimes in my sleep, I could hear him singing to me. You couldn't tell him he didn't have a nice voice. Even when he mumbled the words he didn't know to the song, it was always with love and passion. I would laugh every time but wanted to make love to him over and over again.

When my phone ring, I would usually run to it, hoping it would be my daddy, but now, I let it go straight to voicemail. Afterwards, I listened to the message; it was from Fatima: "What's up, bitch? I'm just calling to see how things are going at work. Call me when you get this message."

You wouldn't believe Fatima held the position she did at her job. She was just so out there, but when it came to her job, she played her position. She was no-holds-barred. Her favorite word was "bitch"; she used it well but not in a disrespectful way. She threw that word every which way it could be thrown, but everybody knew that's how she was.

The phone rang again, and I still decided not to answer it. This time it was Kelly who left a message. She whispered, "Call me when you get this message. This man is going to drive me crazy. I can't take this shit anymore."

I wanted to return Kelly's call but the way I was feeling, I wouldn't be of any help to her. I didn't even have it in me to go get the kids. I just wasn't in the right state of mind. I was yearning for some affection, some sexual healing, or just be held. I didn't want that from just anybody, though. The way I was carrying on, you would have thought I had been with LaQuan for an eternity.

Tima would occasionally ask me if I wanted her to hook me up with anybody, but I wasn't ready to take those steps yet. When I *would* be ready beat the hell out of me, but I knew this sexual tension was driving me insane. I definitely didn't want to please myself. I wanted to be pleased by my man. I'd just lay in my bed and cried myself to sleep.

My phone rang again; this time I answered it. "Hello. Oh, hi, Deb. I'm sorry; I fell asleep. I was going to call you and ask you if they could stay over tonight. Today is LaQuan's birthday."

She said, "I know."

"I can't think right now, Deb. I'm hurting, but I'll get them tomorrow after work."

She was cool about it; she understood. Plus, she loved her grandkids to death. I got under my comforter and went back to sleep. I had to get up extra early—the facility was an extra hour drive. It was a medium-security facility, so it would be a little easier, but I still had to remember they were inmates and to always be on point.

I didn't sleep well at all, but I still woke up with the birds. It was still dark out by the time I left. I arrived at the new facility half an hour early. The outside looked totally different from what I expected.

I was greeted by the lieutenant and the sergeant, and then I was assigned with another officer, who took me and the new officers on a tour. Looking at this place, I was amazed. There were no cell blocks, no slamming bars, just dorms and rooms. Some rooms had two bunks, which consisted of four beds, and some had one bunk. There were even rooms with one bed in them. What kind of inmate did you have to be to have your own room?

That was one side, and then on the other side were the dorms, which consisted of about thirty beds. One thing that was the same was the inmates; they all stared as if I was a piece of meat or someone they hated with all their heart. Certain things were similar; they all stayed in groups or kept to themselves. I toured the gym, the mess hall, and the infirmary. Everything was run differently, even the officers were different. The last facility was filled with a lot of black officers, both male and female, but this facility was filled with a bunch of rednecks.

They all looked at me like they'd never seen a black woman up close and personal. There weren't too many women there, and the ones that were there were white. It reminded me of being at the academy. The white boys would look at the blacks as if we were aliens. One of them even had the nerve to say, "I never saw a colored person in real life before; only on TV." I looked at the bastard, like, *Colored? Who the fuck are you calling colored? This ain't the 1940s or '50s.* I knew I would be called all kinds of niggers behind my back, but those motherfuckers better not let me hear it, or I would forget who and where I was.

Like the other facility, I was taken to one of the units to do the count on my own. I did the count once, and it was incorrect. The unit had fifty-four inmates, but I only counted fifty-three heads. *Do not panic, bitch* — that's what I told myself — *just take the count over.* I checked the list to make sure no one was out. *Why am I only coming up with fifty-three?*

"On the count!" I yelled, and did it over once more, and still — fifty-three inmates. *Okay, these inmates are playing a game with me.* I called the count again — forty-eight, forty-nine, fifty. No, wait — where's fifty at? I checked inside the single-bed room to find number fifty crunched up in the corner. "Hello, excuse me; did you not hear me call the count?"

"Oh, I'm sorry, CO." He looked like he had mental issues, so I decided not to go there with him. I continued with my count: "Fifty-one, fifty-two, fifty-three, and fifty-four. Thank God."

After the count, I was assigned to the yard. On my way walking to the yard, I looked and saw this five foot eleven, well-groomed, handsome man. My heart dropped to the floor. I walked toward him and said, "Excuse me." He had his back toward me, and when he turned around, my eyes started tearing up. "Why baby? Why would you do this to me?" Standing in front of me was LaQuan. He looked like he had seen a ghost, and he turned and walked away from me. I couldn't move; I wanted to run and catch up to him as if we were on the streets, but I couldn't, because we weren't on the streets. I continued on to my post with tears in my eyes. I knew I couldn't watch the yard when I was full of emotions, because they ran too deep. I was so confused and hurt, but so happy to see that my baby was alive.

How could LaQuan be locked up all this time without me knowing about it? I checked the city jails and the state jails. I didn't understand this at all. I went to my post, and I lost track of where he went, but I'd catch up with his ass eventually. I'd get to the bottom of this.

On my way home, I cried tears of joy, even though I was angry and confused. So many questions I had for him. Did he know I'd had his baby? Why was he locked up? When was he coming home? Most of all, why did he leave me in the dark like that? Why didn't he trust me enough to let me know he got knocked? Should I tell anybody? Nah, not yet. I needed to get to the bottom of this shit.

How could my baby be locked the fuck up? Something was wrong with this picture. Even though I wanted to kick his ass, all I could think about was how good he looked. I wanted to fuck the shit out of him. My mind was racing, my heart was pounding, and my daddy was alive. I knew it all this time; I felt it. All I wanted to do was get to my kids, take them home, and get ready for tomorrow's showdown. I needed to find out why he was locked up.

When I got to my mother's house, I was moving at such a fast pace she had to tell me to slow down. "What's the problem? Did you have a bad day?"

"No," I said. I was dying to tell her I'd seen LaQuan, but I knew I couldn't tell her—not just yet; not until I found out what the hell was really going on with him. "No, I didn't have a bad day," I said with so much excitement in my voice. "Actually, this facility seems a whole lot better than the other one. I'm just tired, and I want to get home, and get in my bed—that's all." In reality, I was trying to absorb everything that had happened today. It had been such a bittersweet moment. I looked at my kids and thought how grateful I was to have them in my life.

Before I could get inside my house, my phone rang. I definitely would not rush to get it. It could be Rell, calling to spoil my mood. I had a big day ahead of me tomorrow, and for the first time, I felt good about going to work. I was so anxious and excited; I still couldn't believe what had happened. My heart had been hurting for so long, and knowing that he was alive changed everything. I could finally begin to heal this broken heart of mines — I hoped.

I was up bright and early. I dropped the kids off and kept it moving. It was time to get some answers. I got to work, got my assignment, and prepared myself for this showdown. I worked the mess hall, and I looked at every inmate that walked in there for breakfast, but I didn't see LaQuan.

After that, I was assigned to a unit. When I got there, most of the inmates were sleeping or getting ready for school or work. I looked at all the names on the roster, but I didn't see LaQuan Cummings. The day came and went, and I still didn't see the love of my life. This was making me tear up. *Why the fuck is he hiding from me?* On my way out, I looked around, but I didn't see him anywhere in sight. When I got home, I tried to call his mother again, but just like any other time, it went to voicemail. It hurt me that she didn't let me know he was locked up, knowing I had his baby. Everything became clear to me. *So that's why she was so sick and stressed out. Her son was locked up.* I needed to talk to somebody. I needed to get this shit off my chest. Who should I call? It was between Kelly and Shantae. Kelly would understand what I was going through a little better. She had some experience with the jail life, anyway. Kelly was the type of person who didn't bite her tongue, and when some racist female cop jumped in her face, she held off and punched the bitch in her face. It wasn't even her problem—the cops were there with a warrant for Keith's arrest. This landed her pregnant ass right in jail, so she knew the stresses of being behind bars.

"Hello."

"What's up, girl?"

"What's up, Tee."

"Girl you won't believe me when I tell you this shit."

"What happened?" she said with curiosity in her voice.

"I started at this new facility on Monday and who did I see? Nobody but Mr. Cummings himself."

"Get the fuck out of here! You fucking lying."

"Kelly, I swear to everything I love."

"What the fuck did he say when he saw you?"

"Nothing at all. He just walked away. He looked tight and kind of ashamed at the same time."

"You mean to tell me all this time he has been locked up, and he didn't even call you or even write you to let you know."

"Now you tell me how a bitch like me is supposed to feel."

"Did you see him today?"

"No, I looked, but I didn't see him nowhere in sight. He was probably ducking me."

"Yo, that shit is fucked up."

"Kelly, you just don't know how much I'm hurting inside. I can't even cry. I was so glad to see that he was still alive but so hurt that he didn't trust me enough to let me know what went down. I would have held him down no matter what, because he has been there for me."

"Girl, I can't tell you what to do, but see what he tells you first, before you jump to conclusions."

"Regardless of the hurt, that motherfucker still had me all excited. I just wanted to fuck the shit out of him, and then kick his ass."

Kelly started laughing. "I know that's right."

"I just needed to tell somebody. You feel me."

"Do what you got to do, girl."

"Thanks for listening. So what's up with you?"

"Girl, do you really want to know?"

"Yeah, what's up?"

"Why was John and I about get it on in his truck last night?"

"What John? Keith's friend John?"

"Hell, yeah. I don't know what happened, but I can't take Keith ass no more, and John was that shoulder I needed."

"So what stopped you?"

"Nothing stopped me. I'm going to fuck him. It's just a matter of time."

"You got to be careful with the 'fucking the friend' shit. It might come back to bite you in the ass."

"I know, but the way I'm feeling now—fuck it. Whatever happens, happens."

"Well, I'm a good shoulder to lean on, too. Think about it before you do something you might regret, but I'll call you later to check up on you."

<><><>

Three more days went by, and I still didn't see LaQuan. I wondered if he asked for a transfer. I didn't know too much about how things worked at this spot; I was still learning. I hadn't really connected with anybody here yet, so I couldn't even ask anybody. I just had to lay low and wait until I saw his ass again. *Next time, he won't get away.*

I didn't see LaQuan, but I looked forward to my days off. I was relieved in a way, and I wanted to party. So I called my girls.

"Let's go out tonight, bitches. Let's go to a bar or something."

I knew they were all thinking, *what's up with this bitch? All of a sudden she wants to go out*—everybody thought that except for Kelly; she knew why I was in such a partying mood.

Everybody met up at my house. Fatima was looking at me all weird.

"What's up, bitch? What you all jolly about? I guess you finally realized you got to let go and spread the love to somebody else."

"Hell, no, Tima. I'm not you. I'm just happy right now. What's wrong with that?"

Kelly looked at me and said, "nothing's wrong with that. Don't listen to Fatima's fast ass."

Since Shantae is always talking about the gay scene, we decided to explore her world, just out of curiosity. I still was not convinced Shantae was gay. I think she was on that fade shit like a lot of other people. It didn't matter if she was straight or gay; that bitch still thought she was God's gift to both men and women. For some reason, the women loved her just as much as the men.

If you ask a woman why she's with another woman, a lot of times she will say because another woman seems to understand what she feels or wants. It's more of an emotional type of relationship. Watching Shantae made me feel like women were just as bad as men were. She cheated and made women cry, just like men. She put her strap on and fucked the shit out of them, as she liked to say. She had them spending money on her and buying her nice things. They even told her they were in love with her within a matter of weeks, and deep down inside, she knew she would be moving on to the next vulnerable bitch and put her through the same thing.

The woman's heart was still used and abused but instead of it being done by a man, it was done by a woman — the one who supposedly knew how to treat a woman because she knew how women felt and what women went through.

Yeah, right.

It was all bullshit, but to each its own. I still loved her, even though she was a womanizer. We finally got to the bar. It was all right inside — a little small but cozy.

Fatima said, "Where the fuck is the men?"

We all looked at her like she was crazy.

"Stop playing, bitch. You know this is a gay bar."

"That's not good for me. Who the fuck is going to buy me a drink.?"

Shantae looked at her. "Oh, I'm quite sure you'll find somebody to buy you a drink, even if it's a woman."

"You got that right, bitch, because Fatima don't like spending her own money." The bar was okay; it was kind of strange to see the same sex all over one another, dancing, kissing, and doing all that other shit. Just as long as nobody came at me. I was too cute to be having women grinding all up on me. I needed something long and strong.

After a couple of drinks I was ready to go. My mind kept going to the day I saw LaQuan. He still looked as good as ever, and I was dying to know what the fuck he was doing in there. I was sitting there in my moment when I felt someone sit next to me. "What you drinking?"

"Oh, nothing, thank you," I said. "I'm done for the night." I tried to keep my cool. I looked around for the rest of them bitches, but they were on the dance floor.

"Are you here with someone?" she asked.

I turned around and looked at this woman, who could definitely pass for a man. I guess she was the quote/unquote "aggressive" type. I wanted to say, *"listen, bitch, I don't do the licky-licky,* but instead I said, "Yes, I'm here with somebody." I looked on the dance floor for Shantae. I got up and went to the dance floor and found Shantae grinding all up on some chick. "Bitch, whose idea, was it to come to a gay bar?"

She looked at me and started laughing. "Yours," she said. "Why? What's the problem? Don't tell me you're ready to go."

"Yes, the fuck I am."

"Stop acting up, Tee."

"I guess you're right, but I don't want no woman trying to push up on me."

"Damn, Taraine, you're the only one complaining. Live a little."

I looked at everybody else having a good time, including Fatima. I definitely had a good reason to celebrate, and that's just what I was going to do. I noticed one thing, though—they may have been having fun, but all them bitches was dancing together. I guess that was to make sure no one stepped to them. *These bitches are funny, and I might as well join them.*

Chapter 12

A Little Setback

I was determined to get to the bottom of this shit with LaQuan. I was going to find my man—I guess he was still my man. I wasn't assigned to the mess hall; they sent me straight to a unit. Once I got in the unit, I went straight to my desk and looked on my roster for LaQuan Cummings. I still didn't see his name, so I figured he was not in this unit. I walked throughout the house to check it thoroughly; making sure everything was all right; making sure there was one man to a bed. You see some crazy shit happening in these facilities. Even though this was a medium-security facility, I still had to stay on my toes and make sure I didn't get too lax.

After breakfast, the inmates had a choice: they either could go to the gym or they could go to the yard. I checked the unit to make sure everything was okay, and then I went back to my office. I was deep in thought when I heard someone say, "Hey, beautiful." I couldn't even look up; it felt like my heart had stopped for a moment, and my eyes began to fill with tears. I looked up at my baby; he was just as fine as the day we met. I wanted to jump up and kiss him forever, but I couldn't.

"LaQuan." That's all I could get out my mouth as I just stared at him. "Why, Daddy, why?"

He said, "Moc, I can't really talk to you the way I would like to, but I'll get the chance to explain everything to you soon."

"I looked you up on the computer, and your name didn't come up."

"Did you look carefully at the names on the roster?"

"Yes, baby, I did, and I didn't see your name."

"Well, look again, baby."

I looked at all the names and right before my eyes was *Leon Cummings*. "They got you here under your middle name. That's why I couldn't find you when I went to the hospitals or even the precincts."

He still had it. I wanted to jump his bones, and I guess he was thinking the same thing I was thinking, because when I looked at him from head to toe, his dick was talking to me. "I miss you so much," I said. "There's so much I want to tell you and so much I need to know."

"How's my baby girl, Raine, doing?"

My mouth damn near dropped to the floor. "How you know about Raine? Who told you I had your baby?" I just forgot where I was and let it all out. "LaQuan, why didn't you trust me enough to let me know you were locked up?"

"I didn't want to disappoint you, Moc. I didn't want to hurt you."

"So me thinking you ran off and left me, or better yet, me wondering if you were dead wouldn't hurt me, LaQuan? So what happened?"

"I'll talk to you later about everything, when I know it's safe. These clowns around here are so fucking nosey, and they will try to get all up in your shit, so we have to be safe. When I heard you were working for corrections, I was tight, but who the fuck am I to stop your money? You have to be careful, Moc. You might think you know about this life, but you don't know shit."

Every now and then, an inmate passed and looked at us talking, but I kept it very professional.

"Do you know how much it hurt me to be locked up while you were out there, carrying my baby?"

"Do you know how stressful it was for me to carry your baby? I just knew something wasn't right; it just didn't feel right. What's up with Lance?"

"Yo, when I see that nigga I'm going to body him. He's the reason why I'm locked up, but I told you I'm going to tell you everything soon."

"Baby, I knew it all this time. I knew you wouldn't just pick up and leave like that. I kept telling everybody that I could feel you and that you wasn't dead. They probably thought I was going crazy."

"Moc, seriously, we have to play this shit safe. I'm so glad to be looking at you right now. I don't know how this happened or why, but I'm just glad you're here. See, I told you from the very beginning that we had a connection. My plan was to do my time, come home to you, and take care of the family. When Mommy told me you were pregnant, I turned into a straight-up bitch. Yo, I ain't going to lie to you. I was crying for days. I always kept tabs on you. I always knew what was going on with you and the kids. Just like Lance, that nigga Rell got some shit coming to him, too. I heard how he was disrespecting you in the streets. I got a lot of business to take care of once I get out."

"Well, how much time do you have?"

"I got another year."

"Damn, baby, I don't know if I can do this."

"Trust me, Moc, we can do this. It was all about us then, and it's all about us now. I know I hurt you, baby. I know I disappointed you, but trust me. I'm going to make it up to you.

Everything is going to be just fine once I'm released. Do you trust me, Moc?"

"Yes."

"Do you still believe in Daddy?"

"Yes."

"Then don't worry about a thing. I got this."

"I took most of the stuff out of your apartment, and I took the money from the safe. I bought another safe, and no, I didn't spend all of the money, but when shit got tight, I spent some."

"That's our money, first of all. Any other chick would have spent all that shit."

"Like I said, I knew you wouldn't just leave all that money in the safe like that. Your dreams were in that safe, and it will be there when you come home, but you're definitely right. I could have gone on a couple of cruises with that and bought me my cherry-red Benz. I could have spazzed out, but I didn't."

"I want to kiss you so bad, Moc."

"That's all you want to do to me, Daddy?"

"No, I really want to fuck the shit out of you. You know how we get down. You been giving my pussy away?"

"Excuse me—your pussy? When you left me blindsided, it was no longer your pussy. As a matter of fact, you said you got tabs on me, so you should know I'm a lesbian now; I was turned out. I was so lonely, and I needed comfort, and I couldn't find a good man, so I found a good woman, and trust me—she knows just how to make a bitch feel good—real, real good."

"Moc, don't make me catch another bid." We looked at each other and started laughing.

"I miss you so much, baby. I can't wait until you come home. When are you going to let me know what went down?"

"There's a time and place for everything. That nigga Lance better not let me catch him on the outside, and we better not cross paths while I'm up in this bitch."

"LaQuan, I'm so horny, and phatty is on fire. Seeing you is driving me crazy. See how shit works out? Never in a million years would I have expected to see you here."

"Let me explain this to you, Moc. Do your job, and don't get caught up with these clown-ass niggas, you hear me? They will try everything possible to get cool with you, but they will take you down if they have to. Don't let these COs be all up in your face. You're the new feed on the block for both the inmates and the COs. Trust me; I know."

"Boo-Bear, you know I'm not into that. No white dudes — nah, it will never happen."

He looked at me and started laughing. "You still crazy, baby."

"I'm not crazy; I'm dead serious. Phatty misses you so much; she needs to be pampered."

"Don't worry. I will take care of that problem sooner than you think."

I looked at him. "How are you going to manage to do that?"

He looked at me and said, "Trust me. Daddy will make it happen."

"I love you," I mumbled.

He winked at me and said, "I love you, too, Mocha Chocolate. Don't worry; we're going to be all right."

Time went by so fast, because I was so happy talking to LaQuan. My shift was almost over, and I wasn't ready to leave. Now I knew how they felt in the visiting room when their time was up. I'd just got my baby back, and I had to leave him again. Even though LaQuan was locked up, and he had left me in the dark, seeing him and talking to him reminded me of why I had fallen in love with him. He was a very supportive man, and he was always about taking care of himself and others. Nothing changed; not even his seductive ways. He used to get my panties wet by just talking to me, and that's exactly what had happened today.

<><><>

He said he was going to try to call Deb's house, collect, around
seven o'clock. It didn't take me long to get to my mother's
house. Nicera came running to me, as usual, and Raine was
sleeping.

"Deb, can you receive collect calls?"

"I guess. Why?"

"I'm expecting a call."

At 6:59 PM my heart started racing. I was so anxious. I
couldn't wait to hear from my baby, even though I'd just seen
him a couple of hours ago. At seven o'clock on the dot, the
phone rang. "I got it! That's the call I'm expecting!"

"This is a collect call from LaQuan, an inmate at Green Haven Correctional Facility. To accept this call, press one."

"Hey, baby."

"What's up, Daddy?"

"You got to your mother's house all right."

"Yes, my mind was on cloud nine; it seemed like I flew
here."

"Moc, you know you have to be very discreet about what
you say over the phone, right?"

"Yes, I know. Now tell me what happened."

"Remember I told you I had to take Lance to the diamond
district?"

"Yeah."

"Well, I didn't go inside with him because we couldn't find
any parking. He go do his thing, and comes back to the car like
everything is cool. I'm driving fast, trying to get to you. All this
time while were in the car, I still didn't know what the fuck just
went down. We're about to get on the Brooklyn Bridge and out
of the blue, my car is surrounded by cops in all directions. I'm
thinking, *what the fuck is going on?* I'm cool because I know I
didn't do anything besides speeding, and Lance is just chilling.
They tell me to pull over and put my hand on the steering

wheel. About five to eight cops come running toward the car and pull us out. They laid me across the hood of the car and handcuffed me. I looked up and see Lance on the ground, and they're handcuffing him. All of a sudden, they pull a .45 from Lance's waist and a bag full of diamonds, rings, chains, watches, and bracelets. This motherfucker robs the spot, taking over a million dollars' worth of jewelry. I looked at him, like, *what the fuck did you just get me into?* If I didn't have them cuffs on, I would have done some damage to that son of a bitch. I would have been going to jail for bodying him. When I go to court, the judge offered me ten to twenty-five years, accessory to armed robbery. I kept a little money at Mommy's house, so I called her and told her to get me a lawyer. I made her promise not to tell you. I knew by me not showing up, you would be suspicious, but I didn't expect it to go this far. By the time the lawyer finished, it was dropped to two to four, even though I was innocent. I could see the hurt in Mommy's eyes, but she kept me on top of everything. You don't know how happy I was when I found out you were pregnant, but I was so fucked up mentally, just knowing I wouldn't be there to see our baby come into this world."

I went and sat next to Raine, and I put the phone to her ear. Her eyes lit up, as if she heard his voice on a regular. I put Nicera on the phone. She started laughing and ran off. Seeing this made me cry. I got back on the phone. "I'm sorry. I'm so sorry this happened to you, to us. I knew there was something up with Lance, baby, but I didn't want to bring my personal feelings to you, especially because he was your family."

"I wish you would have, Moc. I go to the board in seven months. All I want to do is focus and come home to my girls."

"I don't understand, LaQuan, why would you leave me in the dark like that. I thought we were supposed to be a team. Don't you know I would have came straight out and asked you if you had anything to do with that shit, and after that, we would have rode that shit out together, baby? You didn't trust me enough; you didn't have enough faith in me."

"No, Moc, don't say that, and please don't feel that way."

"It's true, LaQuan. You put me through hell. I would have rather known you were locked up than have to wonder if you were dead or alive. Do you know what my life has been like? I may not have been locked up physically but emotionally I was. I'm thankful that Raine didn't come out all sick and shit. She looks just like you, baby. I'm so glad you're alive and not six feet under, but I'm angry as hell. What happened to that bitch Lance?"

"I'm not sure where he's at, but he tried to act all disturbed. That nigga is going to be disturbed after I'm done with him. Don't worry, Moc; you just continue going to work and stacking your money and taking care of my girls. Keep my phatty tight, and oh, yeah, you still a bad bitch, Moc, even in your polyester uniform."

I started laughing. "Thank you. I love you."

"Do you really, Moc?"

"Yes, I do, with all my heart."

"Even after finding out I'm locked up?"

"I loved you before you were locked up, LaQuan. Jail doesn't make you who you are. I hope you stay focused and come home to continue with your plans of becoming an entrepreneur. Your life isn't over because you're locked up. There are a lot of people in jail that don't belong there. I can't speak for anybody else, but if you tell me you didn't know anything about what Lance was up to, I believe you, baby, and nobody can tell me different."

"It might not have shown it on our visit, but seeing you took a lot of stress off me," he said.

I realized he was talking in code when he said "seeing you on our visit," which meant the day he saw me by the yard.

"Mocha, you know I love you."

"I love you, too, baby."

Chapter 13

Shutting Them Down

Now that I knew my baby was all right, everything seemed so clear to me, and life was good again. I was looking forward to our future together, a future I'd been quite unsure of. This was definitely a lesson for me, so I'd just live in the moment because nothing was promised to anyone.

I was so happy on my way to work. I hoped they'd put me back in LaQuan's unit, but I didn't see it happening again. *There's absolutely nothing wrong with a little wishful thinking.*

We lined up to get our post assignment and to my surprise, I was placed back in my baby's unit. I guess my wishful thinking paid off. When I got to the unit, everybody was doing their regular routine, either getting ready for work or school. The ones that didn't have either would still be sleeping. LaQuan was still asleep; he didn't even know I was back in his unit.

Damn, all I wanted to do was climb into that little cot and lie right next to my man. Nah, fuck that; I wanted to climb on top of him and give him the ride of his life and to show him I still had it. I know he was tired of jerking off. He had pictures of me and the kids up. He must have got that from his mother, but he had to remove my pictures. *Oh, I could kill his mother for keeping this shit from me.* I understood, in a way. I guess that shows a mother's true love for her child. *When he leaves out to go to the mess hall, I'm going to look through his shit to see if he has a bunch of bitches writing him or sending him pictures,* I thought. I did not stand there too long watching him sleep, even though I wanted to, but I had to make my rounds on the rest of the unit.

Everything seemed to be okay, so I went to my office to write it in the book: "Unit in safe condition." As soon as I finished writing, here he came with his toothbrush and towel in his hand. He looked shocked when he saw me. He smiled and winked at me, nodding in the direction of the shower room.

Oh, how I wish I could, Daddy, I thought as he proceeded to walk to the bathroom in a wife-beater and some red gym shorts. Damn, my baby was hot as ever; he gave me chills. *Can I get through this until he comes home?* He turned around and mumbled "I love you," and I mumbled it right back.

While he was in the shower, this inmate walked up to my office window. "Good morning, CO."

"Good morning."

This dude looked like an old-school crack-head. "You new here?" he asked.

"Yes, I am."

"Well, I just wanted to let you know to be very careful about who you choose to talk to. These motherfuckers in here are up to no good."

"Thanks for the advice, but I got this."

He continued rambling on and on, talking about how the other inmates got down. By this time LaQuan was out of the shower and dressed. I didn't know what he did or said, but whatever it was got his ass away from my window.

I started laughing. "What did you say to him?"

"I just saved your ass, that's what I did."

"Why you say that?"

He never answered. "Didn't I tell you to watch who you talk to, Moc? That dude is a weirdo."

"A what?"

"A rapist, Moc. You're gonna have me in here fucking these clowns up. I see it coming already."

"Baby, he just came to the window and started warning me about these inmates, which I already knew the deal."

"I understand that, Moc, but when they come at you like that, you have to shut them down."

"I hear you, LaQuan. Excuse me, Mr. Cummings, but you can't be the only one I talk to. That's going to look a little suspicious."

"You right," he said. "Just play it safe."

"So ... how many girls' been writing you?" I asked.

"Do not ask me no dumb shit like that."

"I'm dead serious, LaQuan."

"Go check my cube."

"Oh, trust me, I will."

That was procedure anyway, to do random bed checks. He didn't know I was planning on doing that shit when he went to the mess hall, but fuck that, I was going to do that shit now.

"Random check," I said as I walked to his cube. I went to his bed and started looking all through his shit. He was looking me up and down, trying to have the tight look on his face to throw the other inmates off. I picked up a calendar of Buffy the Body. I turned back and looked at him. "What's this?"

He looked at me, and shrugged his shoulders, and started smiling.

"It has to go. This is the only ass you need, right here. So you know, when I get home I'm going to order me a calendar of big black dicks, right."

"Don't get fucked up," he said.

"Whatever," I said as I continued looking through his shit. I saw a letter from a girl named Vera. She was the manager from the club he worked at. "Why did Vera know you were locked up, but I didn't?"

"Don't go there, Moc."

"Oh, I'm going there. Why the fuck was it okay for you to tell her but not me?"

"I had to call her. She still had money for me, and I had to let her know what went down, for business purposes only. Mommy was holding me down, but once I found out she was getting sick, I didn't want me being locked up to be the cause of her getting sick. So Vera started doing what Mommy was doing. Trust me; it ain't like that. You know she good people."

I continued looking through his shit. He had some tapes of Nas, Jadakiss, and 50 Cent. All the pictures I sent to his mother, he had. I looked in a box, and it was full of letters. "Oh, shit. Your ass is done." When I looked at the first letter, I saw it was addressed to me. I just looked at him, and then looked back into the box. There were over a hundred letters addressed to me. I couldn't really talk to him the way I wanted to; it would have been too obvious.

"What is this about?"

"I told you I didn't want to hurt you, but believe me, you have always been on my mind. I wrote you almost every other day, but I never had the guts to mail them."

I looked at him and was about to get all mushy. *Get it together, bitch, this is not the time or place to be losing control,* I thought. I just wanted to grab him and hold him forever. I was done looking through his shit. My heart couldn't take it anymore. I left him and went back into my office. I still had one more bed to check, but I needed to get myself together. I went into my office bathroom and cried like a fucking baby. If I had seen that bitch Lance right now, I would have killed him my damn self. He took my child's father away from her; he took the love of my life away from me; and he was going to pay for this shit.

I came out of the bathroom, ready to do the next bed check. I had to put my gloves on for this one. Some of these inmates were so fucking nasty. I did a little damage to the next room.

When the inmate came back to his room, he was upset. He came to my office. "Yo, CO, why you do me like that?"

"Excuse me?" I said.

"Why you fucked my room up like that? Yo, that's fucked up. You're new around here, and I see you don't know how shit works."

"Oh, it works just fine for me."

"Would you want me to fuck up your shit like that, CO?"

"You can do whatever you like, but trust me, I will write your ass up."

"Yo, fuck you and that ticket."

As I got up to check his ass, all I saw was LaQuan going toward him. "Yo, motherfucker, you better watch how you talk to women."

"Nah, man, this bitch just fucked my whole shit up. Now I got to be up all night trying to fix this shit back."

"Yo, check this out; she did my shit the same way, but don't come at her like that, my man. Just go fix your shit up. Don't act like these crackers don't do your shit the same way."

"You got it, yo," he said as he walked back to his room.

"Baby, thank you, but he's not worth it." I yelled down to the inmate, "If you have a problem with what I did to your room, write me up."

"I will," he said.

"Now back to you: what happened to lying low, baby? We can't afford any problems. I see I have to stay on my p's and q's with you. I don't want to get you into any bullshit, LaQuan, but thanks for holding me down." I had about an hour left before my shift was over.

"Do you miss Daddy?"

"I miss you like crazy, baby."

"You know I miss all that ass up on me while we're sleeping. You definitely know I miss making love to you and putting that ass to sleep. I ain't going to front—I need some of that."

I looked at him, smiling. "You're so nasty."

"No, I'm not nasty, baby. I'm backed the fuck up."

I sat in my office, waiting for my relief to come. Even though my man was locked up, things began to feel like back to normal. I was just seeing my man behind bars. As fucked up as it may sound, I was happy—happy he was in jail and not dead.

<><><>

A whole month had passed and everything was going just fine. I didn't work in LaQuan's unit after that last time, but everywhere I worked, he made sure he found me. A lot of the inmates were looking at LaQuan as if he was a stalker, but they didn't know the real deal. On a daily basis, dudes would come up to me and tell me to be careful and to watch out for stalkers etc., etc.

There weren't too many women working at this facility, so I knew how these motherfuckers got down—or did I? Nine times out of ten, the inmates who were telling me to watch out for stalkers turned out to be the ones stalking me and watching my every fucking move.

I got cool with this female officer named Richardson. We were totally opposite of one another. I was more hood, doing my job to pay my bills and support my family. She was more boughie, trying to make money and do whatever it was she did. I was an extra today, so I decided to go and chill with her in the unit she worked in.

She told me there was an inmate in the unit that looked just like Usher. Eventually, he walked past the office, but he didn't look like no damn Usher to me. She called him to the office and said, "You know who you resemble?"

He said, "Who? Usher?"

He smiled and said, "I hear that all the time."

I looked at the both of them in confusion, was I missing something. I was just wondering what the hell he was locked up for.

"Why did you blow his head up? Now he thinks he's really somebody."

"He does look like Usher," she said.

After a while they found a unit for me to work in. I liked working in the units. Everything was done on schedule and shit seemed easier to control; plus, I knew LaQuan would eventually show up. I don't know how he would always find me, but he did. He was well known and well respected. Whether they liked him or not at this facility, he had a lot of shit on lock. He even got along with a lot of the officers. Usually, when they opened the yard is when he would come to check on me, no matter where I was.

Once, I called movement—that's when inmates had their choice of rec time. About five minutes later, LaQuan came walking into my unit. He wasn't looking like himself.

"Hey, what's up?"

"Yo, didn't I tell you to watch these motherfuckers?"

"What are you talking about, LaQuan? What happened?"

"This fake-ass clown nigga is going around telling people that when you work in his unit, he is going to fuck you."

"What?"

"Yo, I told you how these motherfuckers get down. I'm ready to break his fucking jaw. Moc, you have to make an example out of one of them. You have to write one of them up; let them know you're not the one to fuck with."

I asked LaQuan who it was. Once he described him, I realized he was talking about the inmate who Richardson said looked like Usher. I was so tight, I was turning red. I should have written him up, but I couldn't; it was all hearsay. He was running off at the mouth about something that would never happen. This was some bullshit. *Wait until I see this motherfucker.*

LaQuan looked as if he was just as upset as I was, if not more. If we were in the streets, that so call Usher dude would have got it.

"LaQuan, all I want you to do is stay out of trouble. I want you to come home on time."

As I was leaving my unit at the end of the day, I ran into the Usher wanna-be asshole. I didn't even know his name, but I called him toward me. "I have a question for you."

"What's that?" he asked arrogantly.

"Are you going around telling people that when I work in your unit, you're going to fuck me?"

"No, I never said anything like that."

"Let's be clear: number one—I'm a married woman. Number two—you couldn't fuck me if you were the last person on this earth. Keep my name out your fucking mouth. None of you motherfuckers in here will ever get the chance to fuck me, and if I ever hear anything about me coming out of your mouth again, I will ship your ass out of here so fast; you won't know what hit you. Now have a nice fucking day, Mr. Usher." And I walked away.

I know what I did was unprofessional, but I was glad I did it that way, because it sent a message out that CO Davis wasn't having it, and that none of them motherfuckers would ever be able to get close to my jewels. I was so mad on my way home I couldn't think straight. I didn't want to get caught up in those types of situations. You always hear about the bullshit that goes on in jail, but I definitely didn't want to be a part of that.

When I got to my mother's, she must have sensed the anger in me. "What's wrong with you?" she asked.

"I think I should put in for a transfer, because I don't want LaQuan to hurt anybody in there. He don't have much time left. I don't know," I said, shaking my head. "I'm going to talk to him about it later." Raine was asleep and Nicera was playing with her toys.

"Hi, Mama."

"Come give me a kiss. Were you being good for Grandma?"

"Yes," she said.

I was so tired; all I needed was a fifteen-minute nap. The driving back and forth got to me after a while. That fifteen minutes turned into an hour. I was actually awakened by my mother's loud-ass phone.

"Taraine, it looks like its LaQuan."

I jumped up real fast to answer it. "Hello." I listened to the operator and pressed "one" for the operator to connect us.

"Hey, beautiful."

"What's up, Daddy?"

"You all right?" he asked.

"Yes, I'm fine."

As usual, we had to speak in code. "I heard you went off in the streets today."

"Yeah, I did. Once I saw that piece of shit, I just lost it. I had to give it to that motherfucker, hard."

"Daddy taught you well, huh?"

"You know you did, baby."

"Niggas will fall back for sure now. So how are my girls doing?"

"They're alright. Raine is sleeping, as usual, and Nicera is running around. I'm tired, baby. That driving is getting to me."

"You and Bozo should take turns driving."

"Who the fuck is Bozo?"

"Your boughie-ass co-worker."

"Oh," I said, laughing. "I don't know; I will talk to her tomorrow and see what she says. I'm going to get the kids ready and go home. I just want to get in my bed and get a good night sleep."

"I wish I was there to get into bed with you, Moc."

"Yeah, me, too, but I have been holding it down all this time. I can go a couple more months."

"Not me, Moc. I need you, baby."

I started laughing.

"I'm dead serious, baby. I need some Phatty."

"I hear you."

"Take the kids home. I'll see you on our next visit. I love you, Moc."

"I love you, too, Daddy."

<><><>

By the time I got home, I realized I was avoiding all my girls. I had to call them, one by one, but I saved Fatima's ass for last. I didn't want to tell her about LaQuan, but I had to. "What's up, girl?" I said to Tima.

"Where the hell you been?"

"Working, girl."

"So what's good?"

"I have to talk to you about something, but I can't do it right now."

"All right, I'll come check you on Saturday or Sunday."

"That sounds good; I'll talk to you later."

Fatima wasn't too understanding, and she could be very judgmental at times. That's why I delayed telling her all of my business. I fed the kids and got them ready for bed. Once I laid down and got relaxed, my phone rang. I didn't even look at the ID; I just picked up the phone. "Hello."

"Hey, Taraine." At first I couldn't catch the voice, but it hit me fast; it was Rell's bitch ass. "What's good? How's my daughter?"

"Do you really care?" I asked.

"Yeah, I do. I'm just in a bad situation right now, Taraine."

"You ain't in no bad situation, Rell. If you leave them little girls alone and focus on you daughter, you life will be much better."

"What little girls, Tee?"

"Come on, Rell, I heard about you fucking with them nine-teen-year-olds. You know, word travel fast in these streets. You should be ashamed of yourself."

"Whatever, Ma."

"I know it's whatever, Rell. How would you like it if some thirty-year-old man started fucking with your teenage daughter?" He was silent.

"Okay, then, I got to go. I have to get ready for work tomorrow." I didn't even give him a chance to say bye; I just hung up the phone.

He did not give a fuck about my daughter; his only concern was me. If I had told him to come over now so I could fuck him, he would've flown over here. Fuck him and his little-ass dick. My daughter was better off without him anyway.

Fucking with these little-ass girls, buying them weed and Chinese food, just to get his little dick sucked—he disgust me. Usually, he would ring my phone a hundred times. I guess I must have hit a nerve because he didn't call back.

I was in need of a Calgon moment, so I decided to light some candles, put on some soft music, and take a nice, long bubble bath. Usually, I would take this time to please myself, but I wasn't really in the mood. I just wanted to relax my mind and think about all the good things happening in my life. I was just glad to be over all the stress, at least for a little while.

When I got to work, I found out the wannabe Usher mother-fucker had written me up for cursing his ass out. Before I could speak to the sergeant on this matter, I found out the grievance was dropped. I wondered how that had happened—as if I didn't already know.

They had me in the mess hall for the earlier part of the morning. LaQuan came through, even though he didn't eat that nasty-ass garbage they served them. That was just his way of checking up on me. We had our little signs we would throw at each other. Pulling on my ear meant "I love you."

He hated when I talked to my co-workers; he didn't want them motherfuckers all up in my face. That was his favorite line: "Yo, keep them motherfuckers out ya' face."

Due to the fact I worked at a medium-security facility, shit seemed so at ease. I had to keep reminding myself that it was still a jail. After the mess hall, they sent me to work in the yard. In due time my baby showed up with two other inmates he worked out with. He looked good, even in his workout gear, which was a white T-shit and brown Champion sweat pants. Just watching him work out had me all hot and bothered in all the right places. He was on this bar, doing some pull-ups, and all I wanted to do was pull his sweat pants down and give him good head. He went over to the bench to lift some weights, and there my mind went wandering again. Now I was thinking about riding the shit out of him, right on that bench. *Oh, I can't take this. I got to have a piece of that man. Everything seems to go so well until I seen him, and then I just lose all self-control.* His home-boy Mark knew a little bit about our situation. He seemed cool; he played his position but like my baby said, you can't trust anybody, even the ones that act like they're cool with you. After they finished working out, they walked over to my station.

"Hey, Ms. Davis."

"Hi, Mr. Cummings. How you doing today?"

"I'm good," he said.

"How you doing, Ms. D.?"

"I'm fine, Mr. Mark."

"Ms. D." was what a lot of inmates chose to call me instead of Ms. Davis. I liked Mark; he was funny. He was the total opposite of LaQuan. My baby had a body, but this dude Mark was scrawny as hell. Calling himself getting his workout on, I thought that was so hilarious. In the streets, my baby wouldn't even fuck with somebody like him. My day was almost over. Mark started walking away so we could get a couple of words in before I left for the day.

"Moc, I need phatty, and if the opportunity comes, I have to fuck you, baby. I need some of you, baby. I ain't going to lie."

"Daddy, I'm not going to talk about this. Whatever happens, happens."

"Baby, look at me," he said. "It's going to happen. I'm going to make sure of that."

"I know it probably will, but one thing I do know for sure—it's not going to happen today, because my shift is over."

"Oh, it's over, huh?"

"Unfortunately, it is, but don't sweat it, baby. All this will be over soon, and I definitely can't wait for that. I love you. Be good."

"No, Moc, you better be good."

"I'll see you tomorrow, baby. Dream about me."

"You know I'll find you tomorrow," he said, with this sly look on his face.

"You always do, baby. That's why I love you so, so much.

Just as much as LaQuan wanted to fuck me, I wanted to fuck him, but I knew it wasn't going to happen. My cousin would always talk to me about shit going down with inmates and officers at her job, and I would always wonder how the fuck was that possible. In many ways, I could see how shit like that could happen. Some of these men were to die for. Many of these guys would be a good catch if they were on the streets. Temptation has a way of getting the best of you, especially if you're a vulnerable person. Many of these inmates could be very manipulating; that's why it was very important to realize where you're at. In ways, I felt like I was contradicting myself, because I came into this job with the mind-set of not judging, but some of them will do shit to make you feel like they belong in jail. I know one thing for sure—my baby didn't belong in jail, but unfortunately, he was here. He was the inmate, and I was the officer, and we had a connection no one knew about.

Chapter 14

Needs and Wants

I was working in the drug unit. When a person is arrested and drugs are found on them, they usually say they were using the drugs instead of selling it; in most cases, they were selling them. The inmates lived in this particular unit for six months to complete the drug program. There wasn't too much going on in this unit because they usually were in group or individual meetings. I knew I wouldn't see LaQuan today, but knowing him, he would find a way to check on me.

Usually, while I was in my office, certain inmates would come and say good morning and somehow start discussing their problems with me. I really didn't mind, because it was a way for me to find out about all the other bullshit going on in the jail. There was a lot of bitch-snitching that went on in jail. Inmates would mistake you having an ear to listening as something more than what it really was. Some would even become obsessed with you and start stalking you. An inmate would talk to you, and swear he knew you from somewhere. That's the game they'd try to run on you. That was their way of trying to get cool with you. I had inmates say all type of shit to me, such as they knew me from this club or this project or this school. Whatever comes to mind, they will say. It was manipulation.

I'd say no to every fucking thing. "You got the wrong person," I'd tell them. The best thing to do was to keep it short— "Good morning" or "Good-bye." If you're the type of CO that doesn't fuck with them at all, you become the "bitch." You hear "fuck her" as you pass them, and some even start vicious rumors. At one point, shit got so crazy; I started to feel like it was LaQuan and me against seven hundred inmates. They would hate on LaQuan hard but never had the guts to step to him.

It was time for the inmates to go to the mess hall. I knew LaQuan would be walking through my door as soon as these left out. Even if the inmates didn't want to eat, that was their time to go stretch their legs, smoke a cigarette, and talk bullshit. Soon as the coast was clear, he came.

"Hey, Moc."

"Hi, baby, what's good?"

"You all right?" he asked with a concerned look on his face.

"I'm fine."

"Ain't nobody fucking with you in here, right?"

"Not really. You know how they come to my office with all their shit."

"Yeah, but I told you how to handle all that. I was about to punch one dude in the mouth today."

"Why baby?"

"You know I don't want to hear nobody saying no foul shit."

"Yes, Daddy, I understand all that, but you have to realize a lot of them motherfuckers are trying to get under your skin because they realize I talk to you the most. Trust me; a lot of them are just trying to pick your mouth or get a reaction out of you. Don't fall for that shit; please don't let them get the best of you."

"I'm not going to dumb out, baby. I know most of these clown-ass niggas wouldn't even look my way in the streets. Listen, Moc, the CO in my house is going to be out tomorrow. See if you can fill in for him, so I can keep my eye on you."

"All right, I'll do that."

"Let me go before I get written up for being in the wrong unit."

"Yeah, I'm going to write you up if you keep stalking me, Mr. Cummings."

He stopped.

"What happened, Daddy?"

"You got me all excited. I have to think about baseball or something so my shit can go down."

I started laughing.

"Oh, that's funny, huh?"

"Yes, it is, but you got me all wet between the legs, and you're sending me home like this. That ain't right either."

"I love you, Moc. Yo, try to get that spot. I hope to see you in the morning."

<><><>

After my shift tomorrow I'd be off for the next four days. I wished I could have brought the kids to see LaQuan. Good thing his bid was almost over.

When I got my assignment, I realized they had put me in LaQuan's unit without me requesting it. While doing my rounds, I passed LaQuan's bed, but he was knocked out. He must have been up listening to K-Slay.

One of the inmates yelled, "Good morning, Ms. D." and when I said good morning in return, LaQuan jumped up, looked at me, and started smiling.

"Good morning, Mr. Cummings."

"Good morning, beautiful," he said softly. Once he saw me, he recognized I had on my new polyester pants. He had this look on his face, like, *Damn, girl!*

I started smiling and proceeded on toward my office, giving him the "come and get me, Daddy" walk. Was I wrong for teasing him like that? He was the father of my baby girl; he was the love of my life, but at that moment, we were just on the opposite sides of the fence. This was my husband—well, my future husband. He slipped through my fingers before, and I wouldn't let that shit happen again.

When it was just us and no one was around, he'd sneak a kiss, getting me all wet and turned on, especially when he kissed me on my nose or my cheek. I remember the first time he kissed me on my cheek, the moisture from his soft lips sent electricity throughout my body. The first time he kissed me on my nose, he was trying to get my lips and missed, so that was kind of funny and endearing at the same time. I wish everybody could experience this type of love. Everything I always talked about and wished for, I'd found right in this man. I explained to him that I was looking for "real love"—that "black love"; that Ruby Dee and Ossie Davis type of love; Will and Jada, Jay and Beyonce but most of all Michelle and Barac Obama, not that's real love. I was just looking for that bond between a man and a woman that could never be broken, no matter what. He told me he wanted the same thing, and before this shit happened, that's exactly where we were heading. Yes, I was upset he hadn't let me know he was locked up, but I did understand a man's pride. I did understand he wanted to do this alone and not burden me with all his needs and wants. I hear a lot of inmates talking about what they wanted in their food packages or how much money they needed to be put in their commissary. A lot of inmates were married and had plenty of other women coming to visit them and sending them packages. Women got into fights and arguments because they'd come to see an inmate at the same time, and neither was aware of the other one. Some women knew the men were married but they just didn't care. I could have been that type of woman, so in many ways, I had a lot of respect for LaQuan for not putting me through that type of bullshit. I could always depend on LaQuan; he held me down like no other man has ever done before, and I would do the same for him.

After a while he came to my office window. "Moc, you look good in those pants, baby. They are fitting you well. I miss going out with you and shutting shit down. Baby, Daddy needs some affection today. Please, baby, when they go to the yard, we could go in the bathroom for one minute."

"Are you serious, Daddy?"

"I'm dead serious, Moc."

"I don't know, baby. I'll see."

It was time for the count. I had this on lock after the first situation. I learned how to take my time and not let these motherfuckers intimidate me. I could feel all eyes on me as I passed each inmate, counting heads. I could tell they were looking at my ass. The only difference was they did not have to stick mirrors out their bars to watch me walk. When I passed LaQuan's bed, I bit my bottom lip—that always got his dick hard.

"Count clear!" I yelled. Once everything was clear and the count was correct throughout the facility, I would call for movement, and they would go either to the yard or to the gym. My heart was pounding. I had fear and excitement in me at the same time. I was indecisive on what I should do. My heart and body was telling me to take this man in the bathroom and give him the best professional he'd ever experienced. My mind was saying, *No, girl, you can't do this. He will be home soon.* I called for movement, and the next thing I knew, me and LaQuan was in the bathroom, going at it. His body felt so good, just as I had remembered, as I held him tight. I began rubbing his back; then I went lower to his ass and squeezed it gently. His mouth was so warm as we kissed, like it was our very first time. I couldn't forget about the hooked dick brushing up against my phatty. We were kissing so passionately, but I had to stop. "I can't do this, baby," I whispered in his ear. "You're going to make me lose my job, and on top of that, you're going to get more time." We stopped kissing for that moment and looked at each other — and started at it again. We were out of control. "I miss you so much, Daddy," I said as I began gliding my hand down to his rock-hard dick and started long-stroking it."

"Wet it a little Moc."

I got on my knees and started heading him a little. We couldn't get it on the way we wanted to. Both of us were lusting for each other, and that was just a fucking tease. I left out the bathroom and sat at my desk. He said to act as if he was cleaning out the bathroom, so I made him my porter for the day.

"I'm finished cleaning the bathroom, Ms. D.," he said as he looked at me and winked his eye."

"Thank you, Mr. Cummings. It's looking kind of brand new in there. ...You feel so good, Daddy."

"You do, too, Moc."

We just went on with the day, like any other ordinary day.

I was off for the next four days, and I would really miss my baby. The next couple of days were full, so I knew it would go by quick. The following night, we were having our little venting session at Fatima's house. Before my shift was over, LaQuan came to my office to say good-bye. He said I was leaving him with blue balls. I said, "Well, you're sending me home with a purple pussy. Now what am I supposed to do about that?"

"Go to the store and buy you a dildo."

"I got a couple of them toys at home and trust me; they don't get the job done."

"Neither does my hand, but we got to do what we got to do until I get home. I'm going to call your mother's house on Sunday, so try to be there around five o'clock. I love you, and get home safe. Give my girls a kiss for me."

As I was leaving for the day, all eyes were on me, as if God was sending me a sign that some shit was about to happen.

Chapter 15

Venting

We all met up at Tima's house around 4:00 PM. She can't really cook, so we ordered Chinese food.

"What's up, bitches?" Fatima said.

"I called this session today because I need to vent. Yesterday, I met up with Malik." Malik was one of her side men. "He took me out to lunch and then we came back here. The next thing I knew, we were up in my room, getting it in. You know what my thing is—giving head. I'm a professional at that shit. I rocked his ass to sleep, but I had to wake his ass up, because I knew Charles would be coming by later. I got his ass out the house, and about an hour later, my boo Charles was ringing my bell, and you know he wasn't coming over to watch no damn television. So I found myself taking care of my man, and I had to go even harder so that he wouldn't get suspicious. After I put his ass to sleep, I just laid in bed, upset with myself. I just don't know what the fuck is going on with me. I love fucking; I love making them motherfuckers lose it in bed. I love turning them into straight-up bitches—oh, that shit turns me on. But I need to be honest with y'all. I am tired of going from one man to the next.

"All I ever wanted was one to call my own, and I thought I had that with Alvin. I was always looking for someone to build with, someone who would have the balls to be in a relationship with me, regardless of what I did for a living. I think I'm going to give up on these bastards for a minute. It's not like I'm in love with them. I just like to take them there, and that's it."

"I don't think you should give up," Kelly said. "Just fall back a little, and try to see shit for what it's really worth. Are these motherfuckers worth giving your sweet juices to, and are they worth you losing your life? Most of all, are they worth losing your dignity for? Anything you want, you could buy yourself. You know you don't want for nothing, so I know it's not about what they buy you. You have to ask yourself: is this the life you want five or ten years from now? Then again, who am I to judge? Being married or in a relationship with one person doesn't mean everything is all peaches and cream. I'm in a fucked-up situation where I love my husband, but I'm not in love with him. I'm capable of doing the damn thing on my own; I'm to the point where I don't really need him. I need him to be a father to his kids, but our marriage is over. We tried counseling, and that didn't work. He's very controlling, and I can't take this shit anymore, but he's not trying to leave.

"I don't know what the fuck to do. My kids are the ones suffering; seeing us arguing every damn day is hurting them. I don't want my sons to grow up thinking it's all right to fight with women and control their every move. I definitely don't want my daughter to think it's all right to be abused by a man."

"Well, I guess we're in the same place, Kelly. We are both trying to figure out when enough is enough," Fatima said.

I'd said I was going to fall back and not do too much talking, but this time I decided to add my two cents in it. "Do people really know when enough is enough? I can't make any judgments on anybody's situation because I've been through some fucked-up situations myself. Sometimes that 'enough is enough' never get to come for people, because they waited until it was too late. It's easier said than done, but we all know the reality of abuse. One day, he might hit you upside your head, and that's it—you're dead, and he's in jail—or even vice versa. You might kill him because you're tired of getting your ass kicked. Is it all worth it in the end? As far as you are concerned, Tima, is HIV worth it? Like Kelly said, anything they're buying you, you can buy for yourself. Yes, the love of your life is gone, and you're never going to be with him again, at least not in this lifetime. I think there's someone out there for you, Tima, but you never take the time to get to know one person before you're on to the next one, fucking the shit out of him. If you're fucking this dude one night, then fucking another one the next night, when do you get to enjoy one person?

"As for you, Kelly, I think you're just afraid of the unknown. You have been with Keith for so long that you're willing to deal with his bullshit instead of making a new start for yourself. You know you can do it; you're doing it now." Everybody sat in silence for a moment; it was so quiet you could hear a pin drop. "Okay, bitches, y'all not paying me for this counseling, so I'm going to call it quit and shut the fuck up."

"So … what's up with this trip to Las Vegas?" Kelly says

We all started laughing. We need some excitement in our motherfucking lives. Out of the blue, Shantae said, "I think I'm going back to men, y'all."

"What's new, bitch?" Fatima said. "I might be out of control, but at least I know what the fuck I want."

"Seriously, I'm feeling the girl I'm fucking with now, but I got her open, and I don't want to hurt her. I got these two young tenders from my job, and they got me into all type of shit. I had a threesome with these bitches in my car."

"*What?*" we all yelled at the same time.

"I don't know what's going on with me. I just don't care. All I wanted to do is have fun, and the girl I'm with now really don't deserve this. Y'all know how I am — nobody is promised tomorrow, and y'all may think I'm being selfish, but I'm just living and experiencing shit I never thought I would." We all looked at her and shook our heads. We knew we couldn't do anything with Shantae. She was going through her own thing with these young girls. She claimed to have them open, but I was starting to think it was the other way around.

"Where's the liquor at?" I asked. "And give me something strong." No matter what we did, no matter how we felt, we all had mad love and respect for one another. This was our sisterly bond, and nobody could take that away from us.

Chapter 16

If Only They Knew

LaQuan had three months left. Time seemed like it was flying, thank God, because the same bullshit was going on, with inmates running their mouths once again. After I changed my uniform pants, I think that made it worse. LaQuan came to me and said, "Moc, I need you to change those pants and go back to the old ones." He couldn't take them saying shit about my ass, and I guess he was about ready to get at one of them.

I was assigned to the infirmary; that was a decent place to work. I didn't have to deal with so many inmates. Mark was a porter at the infirmary, so I told him to get LaQuan for me. He came in there and signed up like he needed to see the doctor. This gave us a little bit of time to spend with one another without all the extra shit. I put him at the bottom of the list on purpose. All we did was flirt with one another and laughed at all the other inmates coming in there for their meds. We were like two peas in a pod, and I loved my baby to death. We always managed to bring out the best in one another, even in this fucked-up situation.

After the infirmary, they sent me back to the drug house. I didn't like working there anymore, because two inmates in the unit were stalking me. One was a black dude who swore up and down he knew my family, and one was a white dude who was obsessed with black women. They both were drug addicts, they never said too much to me; they just watched my every move. Even when I didn't work in their house, I would still catch them staring at me, as if they were scheming on me. It concerned me a little, so I decided to let LaQuan know what was going on.

When he came to the unit, I showed him who the two guys were. He told me he was going to take care of it.

"Do not get into no bullshit, LaQuan. I just need you to watch my back and keep your ears to the streets."

"I hear you, Moc, but these niggas are going to respect the game."

"What game, baby? They don't know how we're connected. They just see me as a CO or just another bitch, and they see you as just another inmate who's stalking me as well." I started thinking maybe I shouldn't have told him, but if he would have found out later and I hadn't told him, he would have been upset with me. I told him I was going to be working in the drug unit all week.

"Don't worry," he said. "You know I got you. Let one of these motherfuckers touch you in here. I will kill one of them." In the back of my mind, I felt safe, and just like he said, he got me. "Moc, I loved what happened in the bathroom, but I need some phatty tomorrow."

"No, we are not going there again." But in the back of my mind I was thinking, *Hell, yeah. It's on.*

Before I left for the day, I ran into him. "What did you do to the two guys, Cummings?" When too many people were around, I called him by his last name.

"Didn't I tell you not to worry about it? I got everything under control."

"All right, if you say so. I'll see you in the morning."

"You better be ready. I want to see if you can still handle the dick," he whispered as we passed one another.

"Oh, I'm quite sure I can."

Sometimes this driving back and forth got to me. If LaQuan hadn't been at this facility, I probably would have gone to another facility that was much closer. When I got to work, my sergeant told me he had changed my assignment for the day. To my surprise, I would be working in unit CO_2. I thought to myself, *this couldn't get any better*. CO_2 was my baby's unit. When I got there, I did the usual — checked the unit and made sure things were in order before I let them out for breakfast. I don't know what LaQuan did or said, but it seemed like everybody went out for breakfast. We went to the bathroom and started kissing and rubbing on each other as if it was our last day on earth — besides the fact of us not having much time. He started unbuttoning my pants as I did his. I took my radio off and laid it on the floor. I went down to give him a little head, but he said, "Nah, Moc, I need some pussy." He turned me around, bent me over the sink, and slid all of his manhood in me.

"Oh, Daddy." It felt so good as he stroked me fast, then slow; hard then soft. I felt myself began to release all on his long hooked dick.

"You miss it, Moc?"

"Yes, Daddy."

"How does it feel?"

"Good, Daddy," I said, moaning to every stroke. I really wanted to scream because he was all up in me, but I took it; I took it like a trooper. He loved to see my ass bounce, so I had to back it up on him just a little. Once I started squeezing my muscles on the dick, I begin to fell his body jerking.

"Oh, baby, you got Daddy cumin all in phatty." He reached around and started rubbing on my clit gently. I began biting my bottom lip to hold my scream in from this long-awaited orgasm I was catching.

"You're going to get my ass in trouble," I said.

"And what you think is going to happen to me? They will send my ass way up to West Bubble Fuck."

I started laughing. "You're so crazy, baby. That was so fucking good."

We started fixing our clothes, and he said, "Oh wait a minute. You know I can't forget about my girls" — this was in reference to my breasts, which he likes to call Bubbles. He pulled them out of my bra and sucked on them like a newborn baby receiving breast milk for the first time. He kissed me and said, "I love you, Taraine. It's almost over, and we'll be able to live good." We'd just had a minor setback; that was how I look at it.

We had about five minutes before the inmates came back from breakfast. I did another check on the unit, and then I sat in my chair and thought about what just went down. I couldn't believe I'd just got it on with my daddy, and it was good as hell. It reminded me of our little quickies we would have in my mother's bathroom.

He stood at my door as if he was the king, in which he really was.

"Why you got that big smile on your face, nasty? You are still nasty, and I love it," I said with a smile on my face. "C-Gutta felt like he put on a couple of pounds."

"Yeah, he did; he's been working out every day."

"I'm feeling that, baby."

"Are you, Moc? Daddy picked up some extra tricks while being away. All I have time to think about is shit I want to do to you."

"Bring it on, baby, because I got some tricks of my own. That's it, LaQuan. You'll be home soon. No more Phatty."

"I think I got you pregnant, Moc."

"Oh, you did, huh? Don't forget you got a little girl at home who needs lots of attention. I wish I could bring her here to see you."

"Nah, I wouldn't even want her to see me in here. I'll be home sooner than you think."

It seemed like every time someone came to my window to talk to me, as soon as they noticed LaQuan, they would keep it moving. It was so amusing at times. I know they hated his ass. I would get so happy as soon as he came, because a lot of the inmates were complete idiots. The majority of them would come and talk to me about how they were getting it out in the streets. All type of shit was thrown my way, just so they could look important. Old dudes, young dudes, and crazy dudes—you name it; I saw and heard it. Everybody had a story to tell.

LaQuan would come and say, "You want me to be up in here, fighting with seven hundred niggas over you?"

"No, baby, I don't want you fighting with anybody. I just want you to come home. I told you, I just use them to pass the time. I get a kick out of some of these clowns in here."

"Moc, I'm telling you this for a reason, but you find it so hard to listen. Fuck passing the time. Keep these niggas out your face."

"All right, Daddy. Don't take my fucking head off."

"It's not like that, Moc. You're gonna make me take one of these clowns' head off for talking shit."

I gave him the sad look. "I'm sorry, Boo."

"You know I love you, baby," he said, "and I'll never steer you wrong. I just want you to be careful. Regardless of anything, know that I will always hold you down. Let me go before your relief comes."

While driving home, what had gone down played repeatedly in my mind. It was so good, and it felt so good, but we both knew that shit couldn't happen again.

<><><>

The next day they assigned me to watch the inmates clean the yard. After they finished, I went back to the office and chilled for the day. This office had a little radio nailed to the wall. I made sure all my guys brought back their equipment, and I sent them back to their units. Once they called for movement, I just waited for LaQuan to come, and as usual, he came walking in the office, looking like the black stallion who seduced me on Fatima's living room floor. As soon as he closed the door, we started kissing. I felt him rising for the occasion, and I stopped him. "Didn't we decide we were going to chill?" I tried to say as he kissed me on my lips, taking me there. I gave in, slid my hands down his pants, and started massaging his dick.

"Stop, Moc, you're going to make me cum in my pants."

I stopped and sat at my desk. We needed to stop before something bad happens. We started talking and reminiscing. Talking to my baby really broke me down. I really missed LaQuan—missed him in my life outside of this place. We had a beautiful relationship; we did everything together.

"Who would have ever thought we would be here like this, baby?" I said as the tears ran down my face.

He started wiping away my tears. "It's all good, Moc. It's almost over."

I just hugged him so tight, and at that very moment, I didn't care where we were or who saw us. I was just in love.

They were playing all types of music on the radio. Then our song came on: Mary and Meth's "You're All I Need." I thought every love song was about us, but this one had a special meaning behind it, and it definitely represented us. I knew that being locked up was starting to get to him. The weather was breaking, and all he wanted was his freedom. It was bad enough he was locked up for something he didn't do.

"Your time is almost up, baby, and we won't have to sneak around again. I love you so much, LaQuan, more than you could ever truly know. We're going to be good, but I can't risk this anymore, okay?"

He said, "You're right."

They called movement, so the inmates could go back to their units for the count.

He said, "I'll be back after the count. Remember what I told you, Moc."

"I know—keep these clowns out my face," I said with a smile, mocking his deep-toned voice.

"Love you."

"I love you, too, Daddy."

He kissed me and left to go to his unit.

After the count, he didn't return, so I knew something was up. My gut feeling was telling me some shit was going down.

Another movement passed and still nothing. My heart started pounding. Damn, this was the same feeling I'd had on the day he didn't come pick me up so we could catch our flight. I looked out the window, but I didn't see Mark's crazy ass either.

They called the next movement, but I didn't get out of my chair; I just sat there and prayed, "Please, God, don't let LaQuan get into anymore trouble—please."

Before the movement was over, he came walking through the door.

"Thank you, God" I mumbled. "What happened to you?" I asked.

"I was brought in to be questioned by the lieutenant. He wanted to know if I was involved with any CO at this facility. To be honest, they said your name, and I said, "Hell, no." I told them I got three months left. I ain't trying to jeopardize that for nobody. They tried to run game on me and trap me off, but you know I'm too good for that. Yo, that's my word. That dope-head motherfucker is going to catch it"—the white stalker from the drug unit—"and now these crackers will probably be all on my shit, Moc, so I have to fall back unless you're working in my unit. I'm going to confront that nigga."

"Well, you know he's going to deny it, so don't waste your time. We just have to stay two steps ahead of these motherfuckers."

"Where are you working at tomorrow?"

"Honestly, baby, I don't know. Maybe in the infirmary. I just need you to be careful. You know they are going to be watching your every move, and I need to stay on my toes as well. It doesn't make any sense to step to confront him, Daddy." As I talked to him, it seemed as if he was listening to me, but the anger in him took over completely. I know how LaQuan could get once his buttons were pushed. It was so weird, and at that moment, I felt so nervous—not for myself or LaQuan but for what would happen if he got that motherfucker by himself.

My daddy was a dancer, but don't get it twisted—he lived the street life when he was younger. He used to wild out on them Bx. streets, and he was well known on the streets as well. I guess there came a time in his life when he decided he needed to leave one hustle for a more legit one. Whatever he made from hustling in the streets, he stacked in his safe. I didn't know him then, but I'm glad I know him now. If he hadn't made that change, we would have never met. Shit happens for a reason. People come into your life for a reason or a season, and he definitely entered mines for a reason. I loved him, and we were definitely meant to be.

Chapter 17

Walking into lineup today was a little tense for me. I didn't know what to expect. I didn't know what that dope-head motherfucker might have said to them. Everything seemed to be the same, so I just went with the flow. I wasn't assigned to the infirmary; they sent me to the school building. It was World Aids Day and there was a special program on Aids and HIV taken place in the gym which left most of the classes canceled for the day. I had four porters assigned to the building, cleaning out the classrooms, the bathrooms, the offices, and the hallway. To my surprise, one of the porters was the white drug-addicted stalker — just my fucking luck. I thought my day was going to be smooth sailing — and then I saw this motherfucker.

LaQuan came through for a quick second. Once he seen the white dude, he looked at me with the "Are you all right?" look on his face.

I winked at him to let him know I was good. Due to the fact most of the classes were canceled, there was no reason for

LaQuan to be there, and we needed to stay as far away from trouble as we could.

"We gonna ride this shit out. You know I love you. Just be careful around that dude."

`"I love you, too. Ride or die, baby—that's all we can do is ride this shit out."

"I'll be back later. I need to go check on some shit. If I don't come back, Mark will."

That's all I remembered. Once I became conscious, all I knew was I was drenched in blood, and the white dude was lying next to me. When my eyes were completely open, I saw five to six officers dragging LaQuan down the steps.

"What the fuck happened here?" *Why the fuck can't I remember?* I was trying to remember what had happened. I wanted to say, "Get the fuck off him! Leave him the fuck alone!" But I couldn't get it out. I felt like something was stuck in my throat. When I looked over at Ditmas, the white stalker, he was barely breathing. He had a homemade shank in his chest. I saw a female officer in my face, and her lips were moving, but I couldn't hear what she was saying. *What's wrong with me?* I started to panic because I was still unclear about what was going on. *Where are they taking my baby? No, not again—don't take my baby away from me.* I was finally able to pull myself up to see the lieutenant coming toward me.

"Davis, can you tell me what went on here?"

Everything was still a blur to me. Slowly but surely, shit started coming to me. I remembered sitting at the desk, writing in the book that I had checked the surrounding area and things were safe and clear. Two of my porters had finished their jobs for the day and had gone back to their units. When the next movement was called, I told the other two porters that they could return to their units for the day. When they called the next movement, my last two porters left—one of them was inmate Ditmas, but for some reason, Ditmas returned.

"Ms. Davis, I just wanted to apologize if I made you feel uncomfortable."

"Okay, you had better catch movement," I said, trying to get him out of the school building as quickly as possible. Before I knew it, inmate Ditmas had his hands around my neck. I tried to fight his ass off of me, but his finger pressed against my windpipe, and I started feeling as if I was going to pass out. Trying to fight him was taking all my energy. I tried to reach down for my pin, which would alert the other officers of trouble but I realized I'd left the radio on my desk when I got up to lock the door behind him.

He started yelling, "All I wanted to do was be your friend, Ms. D. You hurt me, and you treated me like a druggie freak."

I felt myself losing consciousness as I tried my best to fight back and reach toward my desk for my radio.

He continued yelling, "You're going to learn how to respect a man!" He tried to unbuckle my belt and pull down my pants.

I thought, *LaQuan, where are you? You said you was coming back to check on me. This white mother fucker is trying to rape me, Daddy.* He damn near had my panties down, ready to take my priceless jewel. *Where are you?* I felt myself gasping for air as the tears rolled down my face. *I can't let this motherfucker get me! I just can't.*

All of a sudden, I heard "Ugh! You motherfucker." I heard someone screaming and punching at the same time. What I thought was a punch was actually the juxing sound of a knife being plunged into this motherfucker. Ditmas fell to my side, and I looked up to see LaQuan's face and heard him yell, "Baby, get up. Wake up, Moc. Moc, Daddy is here. I'm sorry, baby, I'm sorry." He was crying all over me as he tried to pull my panties up. "I should have come back sooner. I should have never left you here alone with him."

I tried to speak but nothing came out. I could feel his heart racing as he laid on top of me. He went to the desk where my radio was and pulled the pin — this would alert the other officers to exactly where I was. "Taraine, I love you. Talk to me, please, baby." He looked at my neck and saw the handprints Ditmas had put there from choking me. "Moc, I'm so sorry."

Hearing him cry like that made me flash back to all those times of being in those abusive relationships with Jay and Rell, all those times being kicked, punched, and forced to have sex. In a different kind of way, it seemed as if I was experiencing the same shit all over again. The man who saved me on the outside from all the bullshit was once again saving me but this time from the inside — the inside of confinement. He held me tight and didn't let go, not even when the officers came. They pulled him off of me, and because I was unable to speak, I couldn't tell them to get off of him, that it was really this white piece of shit lying here next to me who'd attacked me. More than likely, they were taking LaQuan to the box. The paramedics showed up and unfortunately, this piece of trash next to me was still alive. They took both of us to Northern Hospital.

The doctors came over to check me thoroughly from head to toe. I had some of inmate Ditmas' blood on me, so they gave me every test possible — AIDS, hepatitis, etc. You name it; I took it, just to be on the safe side. I overheard the doctors talking about Ditmas, saying they were able to stop the internal bleeding. The lieutenant, the sergeant, and the state troopers came to the hospital, one at a time, to question me more about what had happened. I explained the situation in the best way I could, without giving off any information to the connection LaQuan and I shared. I explained how inmate Ditmas was on the verge of sexually attacking me. I didn't know when inmate Cummings got there, but I did tell him to come during movement in reference to a job as a porter. I made sure they understood that if it hadn't been for inmate Cummings entering the building when he did, inmate Ditmas would have raped me, and he might have tried to kill me. "I don't know, but I'm just thankful for inmate Cummings."

They wrote everything down and left. I called Fatima to come get me. She was a sergeant with City Corrections, so I wanted them to see her in my presence. The only problem was that I had to tell her the entire situation — damn! When she got to the hospital, I explained everything I could remember, and then I broke the news to her about LaQuan.

"What?" she said. "You're playing with me, right?"

"No."

"Well, how much do they know?"

"Nobody knows anything, and I was planning to keep it that way. He was almost done with his bid," I said as I began crying. "Why did this shit happen?"

"Well, where is he now?" Fatima asked.

I don't know where they took him. They don't know what really happened, and they're probably beating the shit out of him as we speak."

"There's not really too much I could find out, but I'll try" Fatima said. She left my room to go find the lieutenant or sergeant. I put my hands over my face and cried like a baby. I was so afraid for LaQuan. What was going to happen to him? All I could think about was the last words he said as he left the school building, about us riding this shit out. I knew he was going to hold his own and hold me down, regardless of anything, and I was prepared to do the same — hold my man down.

Fatima came back but all she could find out was that he was being questioned. I told Fatima that I let them know that inmate Ditmas' intention was to rape me and that inmate Cummings must have come in on him.

They kept me overnight, but all I wanted to do was go home and take a shower to remove all the hate and evilness from my body, placed on me by an animal. All I wanted to do was see LaQuan's face, see his smile, and most of all, see his lips move as he said, "I love you."

How did this shit happen? What's going to happen to my baby?

What's going to happen to me? Most of all, what's going to happen to us?

I just found my baby; I refuse to lose him again.

Chapter 18

Ride or Die

When I woke up the next morning, the doctors informed me that all my tests had come back okay. They were referring me to a psychiatrist, and I was going to be released in a couple of hours.

Fatima came to pick me up. My body felt horrible—every inch of my body was hurting. Most of all, my heart was hurting. When I got home, it was clear to me that I was never going back. They probably expected me to return to work as if nothing ever happened. I didn't even want to go out on comp; I really wanted to resign, but I still needed to take care of my family.

I found out through my lieutenant that inmate Ditmas had made it through the surgery, and that they were going to charge inmate Cummings with attempted murder. I wanted to scream, but I had to remain calm. I asked the lieutenant why he was being charged with attempted murder when he had stopped me from being attacked. He said he couldn't go into details.

My riding partner Richardson had called me to check on me after she found out what had happened. I told her they were trying to charge Cummings with attempted murder.

"What?" she said. "How is that?"

"I guess there was no witness, especially since I was not conscious in their fucking eyes."

"No, I heard other inmates saying Green was there also," she said.

"Are you sure?"

"Yes, they said Green and Cummings went into the school building together." She knew him as inmate Green, but I knew him as Mark. My heart was pounding. I was trying to think of a way to connect with Mark. I called the state police and spoke to Officer Cohen, letting him know there was a witness who had seen what went down. He asked me for his name, and I gave it to him.

"I feel so bad for Mr. Cummings, sir. Please try to help him out the best way you can."

"I'll see what I can do, but at the moment, it still looks like he's going to be charged. You take care of yourself, Ms. Davis, and I'll be in contact with you soon."

<><><>

Every time I closed my eyes, all I could see was this piece-of-shit of a man trying to take me down; trying to take the very essence of my womanhood away from me. Oh, no question this bastard has to get got—he was going down.

I had to leave the kids with my mother for a while. I wasn't in the right frame of mind, and I couldn't deal with them. I didn't want to move; I don't want to get out of bed. I just held my pillow tight, wishing it was LaQuan. My phone rang all day long, but I didn't want to talk to anybody. I didn't want to repeat the same story over and over again. Everybody left messages on my voicemail: "I'm just calling to see if you're all right."

No, I'm not all right, so I'm not going to get on the phone and pretend.

Eventually, I fell asleep, and I didn't wake up until the next morning. The pain was still there; my heart was still beating fast and hard. It felt like it was ready to burst right through my chest.

The phone rang, and I decided to answer it. It was my mother.

"Hey, Deb, what's up?"

"LaQuan called," she said.

I sat up in bed real fast. "Did you take his call?"

"Yes, he said he was going to call back around noon."

"All right, I'm on my way." I was so anxious to talk to him to see what they did to him and what they were trying to do to him. I looked in the mirror; I looked like a hot mess. My eyes were puffy and swollen from all the crying I was doing. My neck felt sore, and the handprint was still around my neck. *Well, I'll do the best I can to hide the marks as well as the pain.* The most important thing right now was for me to hear LaQuan's voice.

Oh shit, I forgot my car is still at the facility! Fuck it, I'll take a cab, and ask Fatima to drive me there later to pick up my car.

I got to my mother's house around eleven; this gave me time enough to play with the girls and be grateful that I was still here to see another day and to see their beautiful faces. Then I sat down with Deb and filled her in on everything that was going on. My mother was not affectionate at all, so I was very surprised when she came over to me and hugged me for dear life. The hug she gave me meant more than any hug I had ever received. Raine ran over to us and joined in on the hugging, and I grabbed my baby and kissed her on her cheeks, making her giggle and smile.

It was 11:59, and my heart started racing with anticipation. I was dying to hear from my baby. When 12:15 came, there was still no call.

"Deb, what time did he say he was going to call again?" I said in a nervous tone.

"He said noon."

Two o'clock, three o'clock, and still nothing. Instead of panicking, I thought, *when I stop looking for him to call, that's when the phone will ring.* And that's exactly what happened. Around 5:30 PM, the phone rang. "Hello." Yeah, yeah, yeah—all that bullshit talk from the operator. I pressed number one. "Hey, baby, are you okay? Did they touch you? What's going to happen to you?" I was asking so many questions, he couldn't get a word in.

"Moc … Moc!" he shouted to get my attention. "Slow down, baby. First of all, you have to watch what you say, you feel me?"

"Yes, I know."

"Are you all right?" he asked.

"Not really. I feel a little better hearing your voice, but I'm hurting, physically and mentally. What are they trying to do to you?"

"Now, Moc, you know they give me mad respect. You know they had to do their job. I'm sorry, baby. I didn't get there in time. I'm sorry he hurt you like that."

We couldn't talk the way we wanted to, but I understood what he was saying. "The lieutenant is coming to talk to me tomorrow."

"For what?"

"They're trying to put attempted murder on me."

I wanted to tell him that I'd spoken to the state trooper about Mark's being his witness; I hoped somehow, he got the word.

"How are my girls doing?"

"They're good, I left them here last night, and I think I might leave them again tonight."

"Moc, do you know how much I love you, baby?"

"Yes, I really do, Daddy, and no one can convince me of anything different."

"It's all about us," he said.

"You damn right, Boo-Bear. Ride or die."

"I'll call you tomorrow to let you know what happened. I can't give you a time, but I will call you."

"All right, baby."

"I love you, Taraine "I love you, too, my knight and shining armor." I was still stressed as hell, but I felt better, knowing they hadn't done any damage to my baby. Assault on an officer — what? They don't play that shit. They will definitely beat your ass while you're up in the box. I felt like a big load was lifted off my shoulders. I just sat there for a moment and prayed. "Please, God, give both LaQuan and me the strength to get through this horrific situation surrounding us right now. I know it seems like I only pray to you when I'm in a situation, but it's not that way. I pray to you every day. I thank you for waking me up and blessing my family. I just pray harder when I'm really scared, and right now, I'm really scared, so I ask that you keep us all out of harm's way. Amen."

Fatima did overtime, so I couldn't go get my car. She said she'd take me in the morning.

"Deb, I'm going to stay here tonight. You can use the company," I said, laughing. Even though there was never too much conversing between us, we had a lot of love in our hearts for one another.

The next morning Tima took me to get my car. She was very silent in the car. She was upset with me because I hadn't told her that LaQuan was locked up and that all this time I'd known he was all right. I just hoped that one day; she'd understand why I made that decision.

"I have an appointment with a psychiatrist today, but I'm not going."

"You are going," she said in a very angry tone. "I'm mad as hell at you, but you need to do everything possible to help you with this case against that bastard."

"I know, I know. I have to speak to the DA also today."

"Don't play no games, girl. Do what you have to do. That bastard is going to get what's coming to him."

The rest of the ride was quiet—that's how I knew she was upset, but she'd come around eventually. We finally reached the facility. I was so glad to get into my car. I didn't need any more tension; I already had so much shit on my mind. "Thanks, girl," I said as I got into my car.

"It's all good. Make sure you go see that psychiatrist."

"I will. I'll call you later."

"All right, chica. I'm out."

I took my time driving back home. When I reached Brooklyn, I decided to go see the psychiatrist they'd assigned me to see. I knew I shouldn't have gone to see this Mrs. Librosky or whatever the fuck her name was. We were supposed to talk about what happened to me at the jail, but this bitch wanted to take shit back to my childhood. What the fuck did my childhood have to do with what happen to me at the facility? After a while, I blanked this bitch out—she couldn't help me. *Bitch, can you bring my man home? Hell, no, so in reality, there's really no use for this fucking therapy.* That's what I really wanted to tell her—her with her nappy-ass wig. I just went with the flow and put on this bullshit act. Black people don't go see no fucking therapists, and I don't want to sit here crying in front of this bitch. She could never understand the pain I was feeling. I wanted to Bobbitt that motherfucker—cut his shit off. What he tried to take away from me, I wanted to take away from him—snip, snip away with the dick and his motherfucking balls, too.

"Okay, Ms. Davis, we'll continue our session next week."

I thought, *No, you will not see me next week.* I left there to go talk to DA Morales. I retold everything I could possibly remember. I told him I'd decided to go out on comp but that I really was thinking about resigning.

"Well, Ms. Davis, only you know what's best for you. I'm going to do everything I can to make sure he gets his just due. As for Mr. Cummings, what he did was very heroic, but the cases will be handled separately."

"Whatever the case may be, I thank God that inmate Cummings was there when he was," I said. "Now let's take this motherfucker through the ringer. I'm sorry, Mr. Morales. It's just that this man was ready to take me out by all means necessary, and I want him to pay," I said.

"Oh, trust me; he will pay. I'll call you in a couple of days, Ms. Davis, but until then, try to take it easy."

"I will do just that, Mr. Morales. I will try."

By the time I got my mother's house, it was nearly dark. I ate and played with the kids. The phone rang. "Hello." I listen to the operator, and then I pressed number one.

"Hey, Moc."

"Hi, LaQuan. You don't sound too enthusiastic. What happened?"

"They added another six months to my bid, due to the homemade shank I used on that motherfucker."

"What?"

"Don't sweat it, Moc — that's nothing. The attempted murder charges were dropped. Right now, it's all about making sure you're all right. I can deal with the six months added. I'll be home soon."

"Well, LaQuan, I decided I'm done. I'm finished with it. It's not for me, baby."

"I'm not going to tell you what to do, but what I will tell you is that I'm here for you, Moc. You are my queen, and I always told you I would never let anything happen to you. I won't ever hurt you again, not even by accident. I'm sorry for leaving you in the dark when I got knocked, and I promise that one day I will make it up to you. One day you will realize I was that one out of ten then, and I'm definitely that one out of ten now. This extra time I have to do will come and go faster than you think, and I'll be home, making love to you like never before. This time, when I get you pregnant, I'll be there every step of the way. Don't worry; just go to court and do your part. Make sure that motherfucker does some time — you hear me, Moc?"

"Yes."

"I love you. I'll call you soon. Kiss my baby girls for me."

"I will. Love you, Daddy."

Chapter 19

Second Chances

Three months had passed, and I was missing my baby like crazy. I had gotten used to seeing him on the regular, but now, all we did was talk on the phone. I made the decision to do what was good for me, which was to resign from the Department of Corrections. Now I was a juvenile counselor at a nonprofit organization.

Today was opening arguments for the attempted rape case. I felt really positive about this case. I knew that by the grace of God, Mr. Ditmas would be dealt with. I got on the stand and for what seemed like the millionth time, I described what had happened to me. Over time, I'd managed to block out most of what had happened to me, but being on the stand was making it all come back. The more I remembered, the dirtier I began to feel, all over again. This bastard was sitting behind the table, looking like a straight-up weirdo. He reminded me of some kind of serial rapist on *CSI* or in a Lifetime movie. He just gave me the fucking chills. I felt like vomiting, and it must have shown all on my face, because the judge looked at me and called for a fifteen-minute recess. Once I got off the stand, my lawyer told me to take a breather.

After the recess, they didn't call me back on the stand. All I heard was "I would like to call Leon Cummings to the stand." When I heard his name, chills went through my body. I hadn't seen him since the day this shit happened. I looked at my baby, and I wanted to blow him a kiss, but I couldn't, so I used our code. I started pulling on my ear, which to us meant "I love you," and he did the same in return.

"Mr. Cummings, can you describe what happened on the day Ms. Davis was attacked?"

He started to explain shit, and I was able to hear things from his perspective. "I was walking up the steps of the school building, and I heard a muffled sound. Upon reaching the top of the steps, I saw Dit—excuse me, Ditmas—with his hands around CO Davis' neck. He was trying to open up his pants with his other hand. I saw CO Davis trying to fight back, and then she just stopped. It looked like she took her last breath. That's when I went through the door, yelling, 'Yo, what the fuck you doing, Dit?' He turned toward me and dropped her to the floor. He said, 'I'm going to fuck this stuck-up bitch. I grabbed him and said, 'No, you're not.'"

Listening to him tell his side of the story tore me to pieces. The tears began flowing, and my heart was pounding.

He continued telling what happened. "When I grabbed him, he turned around, and we started fighting. He bent down to pick up a broomstick that was on the ground, and he came charging toward me. Before he could hit me with the stick, I juxed him a couple of times with a shank that was on the floor. I was only trying to protect myself against him. He fell to the ground, and I went to see if Ms. Davis was still alive. I looked for her radio, which was on the desk, so I pulled the pin. I went back to try and help her, and I guess that's when the officers came into the building and saw me leaning over her. I guess because she was unconscious and he was lying there bleeding, they automatically assumed that I was the one who attacked her."

Hearing him describe what had happened brought back pieces I was unclear of. He looked at me, and I could see he was ready to cry. They didn't know the bond we shared with one another. He explained to them how much he loved and respected women. "I love my mother to death," he said, "and I would never want this to happen to her or any other woman. I could have made three choices: one—leave the vicinity and act as if I had not seen anything at all; two—join him, and act like a fucking animal, committing an inhumane crime; or three—help out a woman who was helpless. I chose to help out a woman in need. I may be incarcerated, but I'm not a criminal, and if I had to do it all over again, I would. I helped her the way I would want someone to help my mom if she was in that situation."

The whole time LaQuan was talking, he was continuously pulling his ear. To the people in the court, it could have appeared that he had a nervous condition, but I knew what he was doing. The prosecutor didn't have much to come back with. Plus, inmate Ditmas had already pleaded guilty.

We went to court a couple more times. Ditmas ended up getting seven to ten years added on to his time. Now, it was time for me to get on with my life. I knew that I would be there for LaQuan for the rest of his time at Fishkill, but I was done with the Department of Corrections—that it was officially over.

LaQuan would call me every night at my house. We would talk and discuss the plans he had before being locked up. We would reminisce about everything that happened to us since we have been together—from the time he seduced me at my party, up until the time he fucked me in the tunnel (a.k.a. the bathroom) in my office.

"I'm in my single digits, Moc." That's what he said when he had seven months left. All we had was the phone. He would even seduce me over the phone. Phone sex was all we had. He made sure he called me every night to put me to sleep—or should I say, he made sure I had sweet dreams. I looked so forward to him coming home and putting it on me.

"I am in my single digits, Moc," he said again when he had seven weeks left. I needed to start preparing myself for what was about to take place. The tunnel was good, but our first fuck was going to be ridiculous. We were going to let it all out, especially me. I needed to go out and buy all type of lingerie and all type of sex toys. I was going to show him the time of his life. I loved my baby so much, and I was just waiting for him to walk through these doors.

When he called me, I screamed, "Single digits, baby! Seven days!" In seven days, my baby would be home. He stressed to me that he didn't want a party. All he wanted to do was be with his family. Up until the very last minute, I asked him, "Baby, are you sure about not having a party?" And he said he was sure—so no party.

I was so excited about LaQuan coming home, I couldn't even sleep. I couldn't believe it, and I wouldn't believe it until I saw him standing in front of me with my own two eyes. I got up and fed the kids. I wasn't sure what time he'd get home. I just knew it would be before noon. I started cooking all his favorite foods: baked ziti, fried chicken, curried shrimp, collard greens, and mac and cheese. Even though he didn't want a party, I still wanted to make him a good dinner. I knew he was tired of that jail shit. I had his favorite drink—Henny and Coke—and I got a bottle of Patron, too. He probably wouldn't like it, but he was going to try it tonight. I got a little banner that read "Welcome Home," and I hung up a couple of balloons, and I got him a banana cake, which was his absolute favorite. I got him a couple of new outfits to get him through the week, until he was able to do his own shopping. Like he'd said—this had been a minor setback.

I turned on the radio to listen to the music and kill time as I got shit ready. After I finished preparing my food, I went to jump in the shower. I was looking sweet as chocolate—his Mocha Chocolate. One o'clock came, and he still hadn't gotten home. I sat on my couch and sipped on some Alize as the kids played with their toys. The doorbell rang. I jumped up so fast you would have thought I jumped out of my clothes. I opened the door.

"Hey, Daddy!" I yelled.

He stood in front of my door, looking so fucking good. If the kids hadn't been home I would have jumped his bones right then and there.

"Daddy's home."

I jumped on him, wrapping my legs around him. We kissed and kissed and kissed. I didn't want to lose this moment. No more sneaking around, no more secret codes, no more blue uniforms, and no more fucking green uniforms. I slid down off him with tears running down my face. "Welcome home, baby," I said, "Nicera, come here!"

She ran toward him as if he never had been gone, and Raine was right behind her. "Look at my little girls." He picked them up and held them tight. He was at a loss for words. Even though Nicera wasn't his, he always treated her as if she was.

I told him, "Go get comfortable; go wash away that jail shit off your body."

After he got out the shower, he looked so fresh and so clean; he looked like the man I'd fallen in love with. We listened to some music, and he played with the girls. He was so happy and excited; it was written all over his face. You would have thought he'd just done a ten-year bid. I guess when you have your freedom taken away from you, and you get it back, you'll treat your life as if it could be your last day with your family.

No one knows what tomorrow may bring. I'm quite sure he never expected to be doing the time he was doing, but he was caught up in a bad situation. It felt so good to have my man back home in my arms; to have my family all together. When he got locked up, it was just me, him, and Nicera. Now we added Raine to the picture.

My phone was ringing off the hook, but I refused to answer it. This was our time together, and I wasn't going to let nothing or no one spoil it. He didn't want a party with a bunch of people, so we just had our own little private party. After a while, we got the kids ready for bed. Once they fell asleep, it was time for the adult sex party — oh, yeah.

I took my shower, and he came to join me. I got out letting him finish. I put on one of the outfits I had bought, which was the thigh-highs with the garter belt, and crotch less panties, with a pair of red stilettos. I dimmed the lights in the bedroom. I had whipped cream on the side of the bed, with the rest of the Alize on ice. I popped in a mixed CD, with all the slow jams on it, both new and old, baby-making music.

He came out of the shower. I hid behind the door as I watched him step into the room, looking for me. I closed the door, looking sexy and seductive, and said in my sexiest tone, "What you know about all this right here, Daddy?"

He turned around and started smiling. His body was looking tight and enticing. "All that I don't know, I'm down to learn," he said. He walked toward me, and we started tongue-locking as his towel dropped to the floor. We kissed like there was no tomorrow. Luther Vandross' "Superstar" was playing in the background. It felt like something from a romantic movie.

"I wanna tell you, baby, the changes I've been going through.

Missing you, missing you
'til you come back to me
I don't know what I'm gonna do."

He gently licked down my neck to the center of my chest. Then he caressed my right nipple with his hand as he guided his tongue to my left nipple. It felt so good. Even though we had our little session at the tunnel, there was no comparison to what was about to take place here tonight.

"Oh, Daddy," I moaned. "I missed you so much."

"I missed you, too, Moc," he said as he gazed into my eyes. He walked me over to the bed and looked at the Cool Whip I had there. He turned around and smiled. "You remembered how Daddy likes it, huh?" He laid me gently on the bed and we kissed some more. There was so much passion in our kiss. He reached over to get the Cool Whip. He lifted some up with his finger and put it in my mouth. Then he took some and placed it on Phatty.

I desired this man; I was craving for him in the worst way. He licked all the way down to my Phatty. He tasted it and teased it and ate it so good. He had me squirming out of control. I could feel my body begin to shake; I could feel my orgasm coming on strong. "Oh, Daddy," I said as I pushed his head deeper and deeper in Phatty. Then he climbed on top of me.

"Moc, you look so beautiful. It feels so good to be laying here next to you. I have been waiting so long for this—to have you the way I want." He slid all his manhood in me and stroked me slowly. "Oh, Moc," he moaned as he gently long-stroked my jewel. "Daddy loves you so much."

"I love you, too, LaQuan."

He made love to me as Jagged Edge's song played:
"Nothing is promised to me,
And you so why will we let this thing go?
Baby, I promise that I'll stay true,
Don't let nobody say it ain't so."

I began to make love back to him. His curved dick was hitting my G-spot; he was definitely taking me there. I was grinding all on him, and then he whispered, "No, beautiful, let me do this; let me do my thing." Once he said that, I felt chills go throughout my body. I began exploding all on his treasure. "Baby, I love you," I said as the tears filled my eyes. I was just so happy to have my baby home; I was so overwhelmed with emotion.

"I'm so sorry for leaving you, Taraine. I promise I'll be here for you and my girls," he whispered as he continued to love every inch of my body.

I just held on tight, feeling every inch of his body, and it felt so good, just as I had remembered the first time we made love. Even after I came, he continued to please me. Every move he made felt so good, so right, and I loved every minute of it. He started teasing my clit, which he knew was what took me there.

"No, baby!" I shouted as I begin to catch my orgasm. Everything began to tighten up, and he knew he had me right where he wanted me. Once the muscles tightened up on his long, hard trunk, he began to cum with me as we held one another tight. He lay beside me, and I laid my head on his chest, playing in his chest hairs as I listened to the sound of his heart beat.

"You don't know how much I missed that, Moc; how much I missed us. I love you, girl. You are my life, and I'm so happy to have this second chance with you. The day I saw you by the yard, my heart felt like it stopped. I knew at that very moment, you were my soul mate. I felt it before, but right then and there told the tale. It was official, and no one can tell me anything different. I want us to live the good life, and you are so deserving of that, baby. When I walked into that school building and saw that motherfucker attacking you like that, I lost it. I wanted to body that clown, and when they dragged me out, I thought I did. All I seen was him taking my other half away from me. When they put me in the box, all I could do was cry."

"Well, LaQuan, I can't put into words how I felt the day you didn't show up. For some reason, I knew you weren't dead. I didn't care what anybody thought, felt, or said. I just knew you were alive. I was so stressed out, and being pregnant didn't make it better, but I'm so grateful that Raine came into our lives."

"I can't believe I got a baby girl. She's beautiful, and you gave her the name we decided on if we ever had a girl. Baby, I can't apologize enough. All we can do is move forward. All the goals we had before is still set in motion; trust me. Like I said, we just had a minor setback, and everything will come to us in due time. I keep telling you, I would never steer you wrong."

I climbed on top of him. "Now it's my turn to show you what I'm working with." I went down on him and gave him that long-awaited blow job he was feining for. I deep-throated that dick. He loved when I spit on the head and let it slide down to his balls. Then I licked up every inch of it—that drove him crazy. I loved to see him squirm and then cover his face with the pillow. I smiled and thought, *Yeah, I'm still that bitch.* I had to let him know that I still knew how to suck a mean dick and rotate them balls in my mouth at the same time. When he was ready to release, I decided I was going to go all in tonight. When he started I didn't even move; I took it all in. There's a first—no, a second—time for everything and that second time was tonight.

We fucked all night long in every way possible, just like before, but this time it was stronger and harder. He was letting me know my jewel belonged to him, and I was letting him know his treasure belonged to me. We rocked each other's world. He fell asleep right on top of me, with all his manhood still inside of me.

First round was lovemaking—that was beautiful. Second round was us letting it all out, and damn it was good. I got real nasty for my man and he loved every bit of it and so did I.

Welcome home, Daddy.

Chapter 20

Da Blueprint

After about a month, LaQuan was right back in the groove. He didn't go back to stripping; he decided he was going to become a silent partner at the club he used to strip at. Vera helped him with the connections—I guess the manager was of good use to him after all. This was definitely a good decision, because the club had become a unisex strip club—Monday, Tuesday, and Friday for men; and Wednesday, Thursday, and Saturday was for women. The club pulled in a lot of money on a daily basis. LaQuan bought himself another Yukon XXL; he had a great love for those trucks. You never would have thought he'd been incarcerated just a month ago. That's why I'd stick to my state-ment—there's a lot of people in prison who don't belong there, and there's a lot of people walking the streets who really belong in confinement.

Having LaQuan home helped me sleep better. When I had a nightmare, it was good to roll over and know my man was there to protect me.

My phone rang. "Hello."

"What's up, Ma?"

"What do you want, Rell?" I hadn't heard from him since I spoke to him about fucking these young-ass girls. My suspicions about him were wrong; for a moment, I'd really believed he had something to do with LaQuan's disappearance.

"Yo, what's up with you?" he asked.

"Nothing. Me and my family are fine."

"How's my daughter?"

"What daughter? You dismissed her a long time ago. She has a great father in her life. Do me a favor: when you're ready to be a real dad to Nicera, you can call all you want, but until then, lose my fucking number."

<><><>

After work, LaQuan came home to talk about our future plans. "One year from now, we should be moving to Georgia." He laid out a blueprint for a piece of land where he could start building his construction site. He wanted it to be in Atlanta; he said it was just as good as New York, meaning big business, but we were going to build our house in Augusta or Savannah. The houses out there were beautiful, as well as the houses in Atlanta, but he always wanted to relocate to Augusta. I always kept to my motto, which was "Go with the flow and never plan," because things might not turn out the way you expect them to, and sometimes you end up disappointed. I also realized that in order to have a house and business, we had to have a blueprint and dream big. LaQuan was on the right track so I believed in this and supported him in every way.

<><><>

I continued working at my job as a counselor, helping young teens who were victims of sexual and physical abuse. LaQuan was always at the club, except on Sundays, which was family day. When I think about LaQuan, I think about the day he told me he was that one out of ten. He said he was going to prove that to me by all means necessary, and he was doing just that.

He changed me in so many ways, and he showed me so many things. I even enjoyed watching football with him on Sundays, but he liked it even more during half-time. That's when he got the extra touchdown, the "super head." After the game, we were laying in bed, talking, and he just jumped up and said. "Let's get married."

"Are you serious?"

"Yes, let's get married tomorrow. We can go to the justice of the peace tomorrow, and then later have a big wedding, but I want you to be Mrs. Cummings right now."

"That sounds like a plan, LaQuan. Wow, you really gave this some thought, huh?"

"I almost lost you once, Moc, and nobody is promised to-morrow. You're my everything, baby—my life, my soul mate, my yesterday, my tomorrow, and definitely my future. You're mines, baby, and I need you to be my wife."

I kissed him gently on his lips and said, "You are my every-thing, baby, and yes, I will marry you, whenever and wherever you like. I love you with all my heart, and nothing is going to change that. *So let's get married, baby.*"

He got on top of me and loved my body down real good. It was so good, I didn't interject. I just loved every bit of it with happiness.

<><><>

For some reason Kelly was heavy on my mind. I felt like I needed to call her. She answered the phone, not sounding a bit like herself.

"What's up, Kelly? What's going on?"

"I'm good. Keith turned himself in for that warrant they had out on him. He has to do six months. So basically, it's just the kids and me. It's so peaceful with him gone. It gives me time to put a lot of shit into perspective. I met this girl name Nicole. I've been talking to her on a regular, and I'm seriously thinking about giving her the goods."

"What?" I said.

"Real talk. I'm feeling her. She's the aggressive one; she's into pleasing her woman. She's from the Bx. I'm digging this chick—everything about her."

"Do you think it's because Keith is locked up so you're trying to fill that void?"

"I don't know; it could be."

"So what's going to happen when Keith comes home?"

"I don't know. I can't call it. Last night, she came over. We were chilling, chopping it up in my room. I was lying on my bed, and she was sitting across from me in the chair. The next thing I know, she just pulled me toward her, pulled down my panties, and started eating my pussy. Keith definitely knows how to do the damn thing, but this girl had me letting loose the goose like crazy."

"Get the fuck out of here," I said. "So are you trying to be in a relationship with her?"

"I'm just going to take it slow and see how shit plays out."

"You and Shantae are on some other shit, huh?"

"I'm just having fun, that's all. I think for me, it's more the thrill of the chase. It feels good when someone wants you the way you want them."

"Girl, I don't know what to say, but if it makes you happy, go for it. Just be careful, because those six months will fly by, and if you catch feelings and she catches feelings, it's going to be some bullshit when he comes home. You and I both know Keith is not letting you go that easy, especially for no next bitch."

"You're right, but he have to come home on some real shit. I don't want all that bullshit in my life anymore. If you can't do the job and treat me right, let someone else do it."

"Yeah, that all sounds good, but we both know Keith. It's not happening, but honestly, I can't judge. Whatever happened with you and his friend John?"

"Oh, we just fucked that one time. It was good, but he is Keith's boy, so we both decided to leave it at that—one good fuck. I've always had an attraction to John. It was one of those things—why didn't I meet him first? He was my shoulder to lean on, and with my emotions in an uproar, he became the icing on the cake. As far as Nicole goes, we're riding this shit out, and whatever happens, happens."

"Okay, I hear you, girl. Well, let me tell you my news. LaQuan and I are getting married tomorrow."

"For real, Taraine?"

"Yup."

"That's what's up. I'm so happy for you. You definitely deserve this. Now listen, bitch, you're getting married tomorrow. Don't worry about me. I'm good. Go focus on you man, and I'll holla at you later."

"Love you. Bye."

Chapter 21

I called Fatima early in the morning to see if she could be my witness. She was like, "Damn, bitch, you better be lucky I'm off today."

"Well, if you wasn't off, we would have just found somebody else, and you would have missed out, Boo."

"Oh, yeah, and you would have a lot of explaining to do, too. I'm on my way."

Before I could blink my eyes, we were saying "I do."

After that, we all went out to dinner to toast to the new husband and wife. Even though it was a quick thing, it was a blessing for the both of us.

"I would like to make a toast to this beautiful bond between me and my wife and to the good life. The best is yet to come."

I sat there for a moment, thinking, *I'm a married woman. I have two beautiful children and a beautiful husband, with a bright future ahead of us. It doesn't get any better than this.*

We dropped my mother off, as well as the kids.

"Just for the night," my mother said with a smirk on her face.

"I know, Deb. Thank you." Even though she didn't say congratulations, it was written all over her face as to just how happy she was for us.

"All right, y'all. It was fun, but I have to go. It's time for me to find a husband of my own," Fatima said.

"Excuse me?" I said, shocked by the words pouring out of her mouth.

"Yeah, I think I'm ready to try this thing called love out once again. I met this man name Karl. He's, like, fifteen years older than I am, but he's so different, and I'm feeling his swag. The sex is good, and the vibe is good between us. He keeps me in check, and he treats me like a woman. The first time we had sex, I held out. I didn't want to bring the bitch out of me and turn his ass out. That motherfucker turned me out; he had me literally losing control. I guess it comes with experience. Nah, fuck experience—that motherfucker is a freak, and I underestimated his ass. I find joy in being with him, and not only that, but he teaches me a lot of shit. To be honest, he slowed my ass down. It feels good to receive love."

"I'm happy for you, Tima, and tell Karl that your cousin said thanks for slowing your hot ass down."

"Well, I got to go. My man needs me."

"Ah, shit, he really got you open," I said, "but trust me—it's a beautiful thing. Now you can work on that baby."

Chapter 22

Sex-Toy Party

Nine months had passed, and LaQuan was stacking money in the safe. I always felt he needed to look into geting a safe deposit box. He said he was going to do that once we got to Georgia. We would be moving into our new house in Savannah, Georgia—eight bedrooms, three bathrooms, a pool, Jacuzzi, etc. It was our dream house. He had already started his construction business in Atlanta, just as planned.

Shantae was having a session at her house—it was a session/sex-toy party. I was running late, of course.

"It took you long enough, bitch," Fatima said. "What? You had to get it in before you came out tonight? You could have at least waited until you bought a toy or two."

I paid her ass no mind. "What's up, ladies?" I said as I sat down.

"We good. What's up with you?"

"Well, I'm letting you girls know that I'm leaving next month. Everything went through, and it's time for me and my family to live the good life, as LaQuan likes to say."

"I know that's right," Kelly said.

"I'm still pissed off at you for holding out on us," Monica said.

"I'm sorry, but sometimes everything ain't for everybody, you feel me? You can tell someone to keep that shit on the low, and they will tell it as fast as they heard it. I'm over that. I'm trying to move on, and live stress-free, and raise my girls in a decent, comfortable environment. Everything I ever asked for or wanted in a man, I found in LaQuan. I mean, it's not perfect, but he's definitely the one for me, the one I want to spend the rest of my life with. I'm not built like you, Fatima."

"What the fuck do you mean by that?" Fatima said in a disgusted tone.

"Come on, Tima, you were out there before meeting Karl. You were free-lancing, and you did it like it was nothing. I'm sorry if it seems like I'm judging you; I'm not trying to. I'm just saying I didn't have it in me to do the things you did."

"Don't get me wrong," Tima said. "I wanted to change, deep down inside, and eventually, I did, but I just couldn't trust these motherfuckers. It's a dog-eat-dog world, battle of the sexes, and I think I was just afraid of falling in love and putting my trust into one man. The next thing you know, I'm falling in love, and with a blink of an eye, he's betraying me. I felt like I was still young, and I had time to do what I enjoyed doing. If it happened, good, but if it didn't, fuck it. Then I met Karl, and he came just in time to shut all that shit down." We all started laughing. "Y'all have to give me a little bit of credit because before I met him, I did slow down a little."

"Where's the liquor?" I asked Shantae.

"It's in the freezer. I just got a couple of bottles of Alize. And taste that Nuvo—that shit is nice."

"Fine with me. I need to get my drink on, buy a toy, and then go home and fuck my man—oh, excuse me, I mean my *husband*."

Some dull-ass-looking woman came in with her suitcases filled with toys and lingerie. This woman didn't even look like she was getting her groove on. What was she doing hosting a sex-toy party? They say the quiet-looking ones are the freaks — the ones that get buck wild in bed — and I guess she proved them right. She didn't show me anything I was interested in; I already had most of that stuff. I just bought another pair of fury handcuffs — how ironic — and some edible cream. I knew my daddy would put this cream to good use, and so would I.

"What's up with you, Monica?"

"Nothing much — same shit, different day. You know how that goes. I'm trying to work things out with my husband. We're actually in counseling; don't ask me how far it's going to get us, because honestly, I don't know. I'm at the point where whatever happens, happens. Right now, I'm just living for my kids and God. He has opened up so many doors for me, and I'm just going to continue believing and thanking him. He knows what's right and good for me."

"Shantae, what's up with you and Deena? You still dragging her along?" Fatima asked. "Are you still fucking with them young tenders."

"Yeah, I'm trying to get to the next level. I'm trying to have a foursome. She seems like she's down, but then again, I don't know."

"Damn, Shantae, I didn't know you were out there like that," I said.

"There's a lot about me y'all chicks don't know. I make it happen. I have these girls wide open. I should open a training school to teach some of these clown-ass men how shit should be done."

"Nobody wants to hear that shit," Fatima said, sipping on some Nuvo.

"Wow, this Nuvo is good. I like this here."

"Then why you listening?" Shantae yelled.

"It ain't nothing like a big stiff dick taking me down. What the fuck can I get from a strap-on? I want to feel the flesh. I love to hear my man moaning when he's about to bust off," Fatima expressed.

"Don't knock it until you try it, bitch," Shantae said.

"No, thanks. I'll leave all that for you."

"Well, I decided to do both. Fuck it—you only live once. Plus, I ain't putting a gun to none of these girls' heads. Either you're with it or you're not."

"So you decided to fuck with men again?" Fatima said. "Because last time you said you were thinking about it."

"Hell, yeah. I am not ashamed to say it. I do whatever I'm in the mood for. If it's a man, I'll fuck with him. If I want a chick, I'll fuck with her. I'm doing me, and I'm feeling good doing me, too."

We all just looked at her and shook our heads because we knew she was dead-ass serious. We enjoyed the rest of our session, dancing and talking shit. It was more than just a session; it was more like "I love my divas to death," but it was time for us to move on to the next chapter of our lives.

Smooches Diva's

Chapter 23

Violate

I was awakened out of my sleep by the phone ringing. "Yo," LaQuan said, agitated. He looked at me with a stunned and angry look on his face. I saw him press a button, then go in on whoever was on the phone. "Yo, why are you calling my fucking house? Nah, nah, I don't want to hear that shit. Nah, that shit was fucked up," he continued. "Yo, do me a favor. Don't call my crib no more, or you're going to have a serious problem, my man."

"Who was that, baby?" I asked in a concerned tone.

"Yo, Moc, you wouldn't believe this nigga Lance got the nerve to call here, like he got it like that. He's talking on the phone as if we're cool, like nothing ever happened."

"What did he say, Daddy?"

"He said he wanted to make sure me and the family was good. I'm so fucking tight right now. I can't believe that nigga just called my fucking crib. He fucking violated me in more ways than one, and he got the nerve to call me like its all good. If he was in front of me right now, I would blow his fucking head off. It's because of this bitch that I lost years of my life. Does he have a death wish, or what?"

"I know you're mad, baby, but fuck him. Let it go. That's why he's still in jail and you're not. He set you up, but you can't live in his misery. He's miserable right now. We need to be focusing on us. Fuck him. You can't get your past back, but you can surely get a grip on our present and future. Before you came home, you said you were going to come home and make it happen. You weren't going to let being incarcerated hold you back. And look at you, Daddy. You're doing it, baby, and I'm so proud of you. Lance calling here this morning was probably to get that guilt off his chest. I'm quite sure he knows what he did was wrong. Now what I think you should do with all that anger is let it all out on me. Release it, baby, release it."

"Moc, you're so nasty."

"I know, but who made me this way? You changed me. I'm now the good girl gone bad. So let's bless this bedroom one last time."

We definitely did that. We fucked liked rabbits in every position we could think of—on the floor, on the dresser, against the wall, and even in the window. We were just banging each other out. I love when we let it all out, when he sweat this perm out. But I always tell him, "When you sweat my perm out, make sure you leave my money on the dresser. I have to keep my hair tight at all times." We both fell back to sleep. By the time I woke up, it was one o'clock in the afternoon.

LaQuan came into the bedroom and kissed me on my forehead. "Hey, beautiful."

"Hey, Daddy. Why didn't you wake me up?"

"Why?" he said.

"I was going to get the kids and bring them home."

"You should let them stay with Deb. They can't really move around in here with all these boxes."

"You're right." I turned and looked on the dresser and started laughing. "You're so crazy, Daddy. Is that for my hair, Mr.
Perm-Sweater?"

"Yes, Moc."

"I guess I'll be going to the salon."

He came and kissed me. "I love you. I'm going down to the
club. I'll see you in a couple of hours."

"All right, Daddy." I got up to walk him to the door. "The
good life, huh?" I said.

"You know it, Mrs. Cummings. It's all about us living the
good life."

"It sure is. I love you," I said as I closed the door.

Chapter 24

Where's Da Cash At?

As soon as I was about to get in the shower, the doorbell rang. I walked to the door, yelling, "Daddy, why don't you use your keys?" I opened the door—and all I felt was a hard blow to my face. I fell to the ground, face-first. As I tried to move, I felt the pain from his boot as he continuously kicked me in my side. I was trying to get up on my knees.

"Where's the money, bitch?" I heard this deep voice shout. "Where's the fucking safe?"

I was trying to catch the voice, but I was in a daze. I fell back to the ground, and he yelled again, "Where the fuck is the safe?" He pulled me back by my hair, and his voice came to me. He kicked me over with his boot, pushing me on my back.

"What are you doing, Lance?"

"Shut the fuck up. Where's the safe?"

"What safe, Lance?"

"Don't play stupid with me, bitch. The safe Q keeps his money in.

Get up bitch!" he yelled as he pulled me up by my hair.

"Lance, why are you doing this? You know this ain't right."

He pointed a sharp object toward my back. "You think I haven't heard about Q up in jail, doing his thing out here? News travels fast in jail."

"Well, there's no safe here. As you can see, we're packing to move. Why would the safe be here? Why are you doing this to your family? Haven't you done enough? LaQuan held you down when you came out here, and you put him in a fucked-up predicament, causing him to get locked up."

"Shut up, bitch," he shouted and hit me in the head with the gun or some type of blunt object.

I fell to the ground and laid there. I could feel the blood gushing from the back of my head. I heard him going through all the boxes in the living room; then he went into the bedroom and threw shit around. I couldn't move at all; the pain from the hit on my head was excruciating. All I wanted to do was get to my phone. Everything was packed away, so I couldn't get to my butcher knife, even if I'd wanted to.

"All I hear about is how Q came home, doing big things. He's doing this, he's doing that. Who the fuck is he? That nigga always thought he was better than a motherfucker, but guess what? I'm going to take all this from him. I called your stupid-ass man, or should I say your husband," he said in a girlish-type voice, "to apologize to the motherfucker and he blew me off. Fuck that nigga. Bitch, if you don't tell me where the money is, I'm going to blow your fucking head off."

"Lance, LaQuan don't have any money here. He invested it into his business," I slurred out."

"Well, you better come up with something. Where's that 5K rock he bought you?" He lifted my finger, slid off my wedding ring, and said, "I could definitely get some cash for this here. You know, I never liked your stuck-up ass anyway. I told Q to leave you, but he was opened off your stuck-up ass. Your pussy probably whack anyway, bitch." Then he started kicking me harder and harder in my ribs. I felt like I was going to pee on myself. Before he could get out another kick, I heard a loud *Boom* "What the fuck you doing, nigga?" When LaQuan hit him, he knocked the gun out of his hand, and it flew across the floor. They begin fighting, and as they fought I tried to slide my body over to where the gun was. It was so close but seemed so far. As they fought, they kicked over the boxes in the living room.

It seemed like it took a lifetime, but I finally got the gun. They both were fighting hard, beating the shit out of one another. Somehow, LaQuan fell to the ground, and Lance started kicking him the same way he'd kicked me.

I pointed that .45 at Lance, closed my left eye, and busted off one shot. This caused him to fall a little. He turned toward me and started to charge me. I closed my left eye again, and this time I let it all out—blow, blow, blow, blow, blow until the chamber was empty, and he fell to the ground right in front of me. I walked over to LaQuan, holding my side. "LaQuan, get up. Get up, Daddy." I pulled him up, and he saw Lance lying on the floor in a pool of blood, shot the fuck up.

"Oh, shit, Moc, what the fuck?"

"The training in the academy paid off, Daddy. This bastard was beating the shit out of me before you came. He kept going on and on about the money in the safe."

"When I got to my truck, I realized I had left the keys in my other jacket. I heard a voice and saw the door was slightly open. Yo, give me the gun."

"Why, baby?"

"Just give me the gun, and call 9-1-1."

I passed him the gun, but before I could dial 9-1-1 on his cell phone, the cops burst through the door with their guns pulled. "Drop the gun, and put your hands over your head!" one cop yelled. LaQuan dropped the gun. They immediately came and put the cuffs on him and read him his rights.

"Wait a minute!" I yelled. "How are you going to read him his rights when you don't even know what the fuck happened here?"

One of the cops went to Lance and felt his pulse. "He's DOA," one cop said.

"Excuse me, ma'am. About face and place your hands on the back of your head." Then he placed the cuffs on me. LaQuan looked at me and mumbled, "Don't say shit," and that was his way of saying, "Ride or die."

They took both of us down to the precinct and put us in different questioning rooms. The first thing I said was "Where's my lawyer? I'm not saying shit without my lawyer."

Someone finally came to represent LaQuan and me. I explained everything to him. He left me for a good half an hour, and when he returned he said that LaQuan had admitted to killing Lance.

"What? Why did he do that?" I just burst out crying. "No, please don't let him do that. We have our whole future ahead of us. We just got our new house, and he just started his new business. Check the record. Lance was just released from prison today, and he came to our home. He violated us. I can't have my life stripped away from me again by the same man who is now dead. Mister, LaQuan is my life. I don't know where I would be right now if it wasn't for him. I have to be honest with you: LaQuan saved my life once before, when I was almost raped. Now, he saved me again from his cousin Lance, who tried to kill me. No, I can't lose him."

"It's too late. Mr. Briggs said he already confessed, and he will be going before a judge soon."

<><><>

They released me the next morning but they kept LaQuan. I called Fatima and Debra, letting them know what went down. I had to call the movers to postpone the moving; plus, they had our shit on lock for evidence. I went to stay with Debra and from there; we would leave to go to the courthouse together.

They called him out ten minutes after we got there. "LaQuan Cummings, how do you plead?" the judge asked.

"I plead guilty."

"After seeing all the evidence, and with your guilty plea, I sentence you to twenty-five years to life without the possibility of parole."

"No, LaQuan!" I screamed. "No, Judge, please don't take my baby away from me. Don't take my kids' father away from them. All my life, I prayed for my king. I finally got him, and you want to take him away. It was me—I did it. He was just trying to protect me. I killed that bastard. LaQuan, please, Daddy don't do this. Tell them." I was crying on the inside and outside because I realized he was about to go to jail for life—for me. I thought about the times when he would say that he was that one out of ten, and he would do anything to prove that to me. I couldn't go on without him. He was my life. I reached out to him, "*No*, LaQuan! Please, baby tell them the truth." I kissed him on his face, crying hysterically, as the officers tried their best to restrain me.

He started yelling, trying to calm me down. "Moc! Moc! Moc!" he yelled. "Moc, wake up, baby."

I jumped up out of my sleep. "What happened, Daddy?"

"You were having a nightmare, I guess. You kept screaming, 'Take me! Take me! I did it.' What did you do, baby?"

I just grabbed him and held him tight. I was feeling so overwhelmed by this nightmare—a nightmare that felt so real. "Oh, Daddy, you don't want to know. I just can't wait until morning to leave all this behind and to start our future together."

"This is only the beginning, Moc, only the beginning."

I hugged him so tightly, looking up and thanking God for the life I had and for my family that he had blessed me with. That dream opened my eyes to how things can be stripped away from you in a matter of seconds—your livelihood, your spouse, your children, your happiness, and your freedom. I'm going to treasure and respect all that I have in my life right now.

"I love you, baby, and always know: I would die for you."
And then the doorbell rang ... *ding-dong*.

About the Author

Inspiring, prolific and courageous; Mahagony Redd defines the dynamic voices behind the women of Stripped by Love. Mahagony Redd was born and raised in Brooklyn, New York. She attended the College of New Rochelle where she received her B.A., in Psychology. Mahagony Redd uses her personal and professional experiences to unleash her premiere novel Stripped by Love. She is also a former officer of the NYSDOC and a former employee for NYPD. She resides in Brooklyn, New York with her two children Maliya and Derrick Grinnage.

Coming Soon:

Stripped by Love II

Love Pain & Consequences